FARMING ENCYCLOPEDIAS

THE 4-H AND FFA ENCYCLOPEDIA

BY KERRY DINMONT

Encyclopedias

An Imprint of Abdo Reference

abdobooks.com

TABLE OF CONTENTS

TD

THE NEXT GENERATION OF FARMERS

In the United States, families own and run 98 percent of farms. A majority of family farm owners are nearing retirement age. This means that new, young farmers are needed to keep the nation's agricultural industry going.

Two organizations, 4-H and Future Farmers of America (FFA), help encourage and prepare young people to pursue jobs in agriculture. Programs in both of these organizations are available to youth across the country. People from rural, suburban, and urban areas participate in these organizations. The programs educate students about the importance of agriculture and help them learn how to advocate for it.

Students in these programs get hands-on experience with various aspects of agriculture. They may drive tractors or raise crops and livestock. Competitions can motivate students to pursue excellence in agriculture. Programs also help students develop public speaking skills, organizational skills, and more.

Agricultural workers are crucial to feeding Americans. They also help the US economy. In 2021, 2.6 million people worked on farms. Broader agriculture- and food-related industries provided 19.6 million additional jobs. In 2022, the United States exported more than $196 billion of agricultural products.

People have practiced agriculture in what is now the United States for thousands of years. American Indians domesticated many native plants, including sunflowers, beans, and squash. They grew these crops for food. When Europeans arrived, they introduced pigs, cattle, sheep, wheat, rice, and more.

People continued to farm a variety of foods to feed their families and to sell for profit. Today 4-H and FFA work to further the legacy of US agriculture. These organizations aim to create a bright future for farming in the United States.

FFA's iconic blue jacket is a famous symbol of membership in the organization. More than 80,000 jackets are sold each year.

THE HISTORY OF 4-H

In the 1860s, the US government gave states land to use for agricultural research. Researchers began improving agricultural methods such as soil testing and seed selection. They also developed new crop varieties that produced larger harvests. However, most farmers were reluctant to adopt the new practices. They didn't want to risk losing a harvest if the new practices failed.

The late 1800s brought many exciting advances in the science and technology of farming.

Youth have always been closely involved with chores and other work on family farms. Joining clubs helped them learn the latest agricultural methods.

Young people were more interested in the new methods. In the early 1900s, they started youth agricultural clubs in the Midwest. These clubs would give students hands-on experience with the latest practices. Club organizers hoped that students' parents would see the success and begin using the new methods on their farms.

A school district superintendent, A. B. Graham, started the first of these clubs in Springfield, Ohio, in 1902. Boys and girls were both part of the club. Club members grew corn. They tested soil acidity to see if it was right for crop growth.

Soon after, Jessie Field Shambaugh started another club in Clarinda, Iowa. She wanted to reward club members who strove for excellence, so in 1910, she made a pin. The pin was the shape of a three-leaf clover. Each leaf had an *H* in it. The *H*s stood for head, hands, and heart. She later added another leaf to the pin, making a four-leaf clover. This new leaf stood for home, but later it was changed to health. Other clubs adopted Shambaugh's pin.

Jessie Field Shambaugh was born in Iowa in 1881.

Clubs began springing up in other rural areas. In these clubs, boys learned about growing crops and raising livestock. Their clubs were often called Corn Clubs or Pig Clubs. Girls learned about raising children, cooking and canning, and hosting guests. Their clubs were

Members of canning clubs put on demonstrations at state and county fairs.

called Tomato Clubs or Canning Clubs. In 1911, the top-ranked boys in Corn Clubs and Pig Clubs produced more than five times the amount of corn per acre than the national average on farms. This persuaded many parents to try new growing methods and crop varieties.

Showing livestock has been a part of 4-H since the organization's earliest years.

BECOMING 4-H

In 1912, people began calling the clubs 4-H clubs after the clover pin. Two years later, in 1914, a national 4-H organization formed. The US Congress passed the Smith-Lever Act of 1914. This act formed the Cooperative Extension Service, which created a partnership between the US Department of Agriculture (USDA) and state and local governments. The 4-H organization became part of the Cooperative Extension Service's education program. The service began providing

funding to 4-H. As a result, 4-H became a national program.

During World War I (1914–1918), gardening and canning became popular activities in cities due to wartime food needs. People formed urban clubs to focus on gardening and canning. For example, leaders in Portland, Oregon, created clubs that worked alongside the city's schools.

Government posters encouraged Americans to grow their own food during World War I, giving agricultural clubs a bigger role in urban life.

By 1918, 4-H clubs had gone international. That year, Sweden started its own 4-H clubs. Other nations would start 4-H clubs over the following decades.

The first National 4-H Camp was held in Washington, DC, in 1927. About 275 club members from 41 states camped on the USDA lawn. Participants had to be at least 15 years old and have been part of a club for at least three years. The event lasted a week, and attendees listened to lectures and speeches from government officials. Students developed friendships with youth from other states who were interested in agriculture.

Leaders of 4-H also met to discuss the future goals of the program. They adopted the 4-H pledge at this camp. Written by Kansas 4-H leader Otis Hall, it read, "I pledge my head to clearer thinking, my heart to greater loyalty, my hands to larger service, and my health to better living, for my club, my community and my country." Later the words "and to my world" were added to the end of the pledge.

The 1929 National 4-H Camp brought 153 delegates to Washington, DC. They were from 41 states and Hawaii, which was a territory at the time.

Events such as pie-eating contests were held at 4-H fairs in the 1930s.

GROWTH

By 1936, 4-H had one million members in the United States. During World War II (1939–1945), more 4-H clubs opened in cities. Once again, they focused on supporting the war effort. Clubs helped people learn how to grow food for the nation. Alongside other Americans, 4-H members started victory gardens. Students grew fruits and vegetables in backyards or neighborhood plots. They could eat some of the produce right away and preserve the rest through canning. This allowed more of the resources of the agricultural industry to be directed toward the war effort.

Boys grew or raised most of the food. In 1942 alone, 4-H members raised 6.5 million chickens and 300,000 hogs. Girls made clothes by hand and repaired sewing machines, since new products were often unavailable. This was because resources were directed to the war. Girls made mittens, shirts, and nightdresses. In Pennsylvania, a girls' club made and folded nearly 25,000 bandages for a hospital.

Victory gardens gave urban children a way to contribute to the war effort during World War II.

4-H clubs in the 1940s encouraged drinking milk for good health.

Clubs also emphasized patriotism during this time. With the earnings from products sold, many club members purchased war bonds. These are like loans from private citizens to the national government. The government would repay these bonds after the war. Members of 4-H purchased $6 million in war bonds or stamps. Even as war stressed the nation's resources and many young men were fighting overseas, 4-H club membership continued to grow, reaching 1.5 million by the end of 1942.

After the war, 4-H saw big changes. Starting in the late 1940s, boys and girls had much more freedom to choose projects that had previously been done mostly by the opposite sex. Gender divisions continued fading throughout the 1960s.

At the same time, 4-H worked on urban expansion. As a result, the organization's emphasis shifted from agriculture to focus more on the personal growth and development of its members. Projects expanded to help members become responsible and productive citizens.

Boys and girls attended the same 4-H classroom meetings in the 1940s.

BREAKING BARRIERS

Although the organization was breaking down some divisions, others remained. While this was not an official policy of the national organization during 4-H's early decades, many clubs were largely segregated. Hundreds of 4-H members attended the National 4-H Camp in Washington, DC, in 1946. But no Black youth were at the event. Many directors refused to send them to the camp.

In North Carolina, Black colleges and extension agents ran Black 4-H clubs. Extension agents are university employees who help create and run programs for the public. However, Black colleges and agents were under the control of white state leaders, some of whom discriminated against Black people. In general, the Black clubs had much less funding than the white clubs.

For decades, Black 4-H members attended separate clubs and camps from white members.

The produce grown by young Black farmers was set apart at exhibitions and competitions.

Despite these challenges, Black agents were able to use their leadership roles in 4-H to reach out to state leaders. The agents advocated for better conditions for Black farmers. Black farming families often had unsafe housing, poor access to a variety of foods, and low high school graduation rates because of the need to work.

In addition to raising awareness, Black agents used 4-H projects to improve the diets of Black farmers. These projects included growing vegetable gardens and raising dairy cattle. They also held an annual Fix-It Week to carry out repairs on farms. These projects helped improve the lives of club members and their families.

Black youth in 4-H showed off their cattle at events such as the Navarro County Fair in Texas.

Black 4-H students faced discrimination at the national level. By 1947, no Black students had been chosen to attend the annual National 4-H Camp. A number of 4-H leaders argued that there should be a national camp held in Washington, DC, for Black students. This would give them the same opportunities as white students. While this did not happen, local leaders established regional Black 4-H camps in their communities. The first was held in Baton Rouge, Louisiana, in 1948. There were 82 students at the camp.

At an event in Prairie View, Texas, Black 4-H members viewed a demonstration about snakes hosted by a state extension leader.

Schools were desegregated in the mid-1950s, but 4-H remained divided by race for several more years.

Participants listened to speeches, visited farms in the region, and discussed the farming practices of the South.

In 1954, the US Supreme Court ruled in the case *Brown v. Board of Education* that the segregation of public schools was unconstitutional. However, segregation still continued in many 4-H clubs due to USDA extension officials who resisted demands to promote national events to Black members. In 1957, the National 4-H Camp was renamed the National 4-H Conference.

4-H members showed off their poultry at the Victoria County courthouse in Texas.

1960s–1980s

The Civil Rights Act of 1964 made segregation illegal across the United States. At that time, only two Black students had ever been to a national 4-H event. But rather than causing white and non-white clubs to join forces, this change resulted in many Black 4-H clubs simply shutting down. This was partially because 4-H clubs in some states were starting to be based in communities rather than linked to schools. Black people often lived in different neighborhoods from white people, so community clubs were located in majority-white or majority-Black areas. Community clubs were required to accept any student, but they usually did not get applicants from other neighborhoods. And unlike schools, clubs were not required to intentionally seek out members of another race.

4-H members accepted honor awards at the State Fair of Texas.

In the mid-1960s, 4-H organizers recognized that the number of agricultural jobs was decreasing. Additionally, more women were entering the workforce. As a result of these shifts, the organization formally ended gender divisions in clubs and projects. But in some states, this change wasn't complete until the 1970s. The national membership peaked at 7.5 million during this decade.

The 1980s saw changes in how students experienced 4-H. Computers and other new

By the 1970s, young women found more opportunities in 4-H.

technologies were emerging. These advances began to change many parts of everyday life, including agriculture. Members of 4-H explored how these technologies could be used in their programs.

Computer technology gave farmers new ways to organize their farms, track data over time, and share information with others.

In 1999, 4-H members worked alongside volunteers from other local organizations to build a home in just five days at the Minnesota State Fair.

RECENT HISTORY

In the early 2000s, 4-H organized a program called the National Conversation on Youth Development in the 21st Century. Starting in September 2001, 4-H held discussions in most of the nation's 3,067 counties. Citizens discussed how to improve their local communities.

These discussions were turned into a national report that was presented to President George W. Bush in April 2002. The 4-H organization used this report to help shape its programs over the next decades. It aimed to help involve youth in government decisions, promote multicultural acceptance, support a variety of learning styles, and more. Today, the 4-H organization continues to educate youth and provide programs.

In 2013, members of a 4-H club in Alabama planted trees in an area that had been hit by a tornado.

THE PEOPLE OF 4-H

The national 4-H organization is large. More than six million students participate in 4-H. There are approximately 500,000 volunteers and 3,500 employees who keep the organization running.

The youth of 4-H today do many of the same things that 4-H members did a century ago.

The 4-H organization welcomes members from a wide range of ages.

The organization is open to youth in kindergarten through what 4-H calls grade 13. This is one year out of high school. To enroll in grade 13 for 4-H, students must have been 4-H members during their senior year of high school. Club members come from rural, suburban, and urban areas. Members who live in rural areas make up 43 percent of 4-H participants. Suburban participants make up 27 percent, and 30 percent are in urban areas. About 52 percent of members are female, while 48 percent are male.

4-H members in Minnesota do projects on a wide variety of topics and create poster boards to present their work. The public can view these projects at the Minnesota State Fair.

There are many reasons people choose to participate in 4-H. The organization emphasizes agriculture, so it appeals to students who live on farms and students who are interested in learning about farming. But it also covers science, technology, clothing, photography, and more. The opportunity to learn about all these different things through hands-on projects attracts many students beyond those with agriculture interests.

The 4-H organization also works to help students develop leadership skills. It encourages youth to be curious and confident. It helps them develop a good work ethic. These skills prepare youth to become successful adults.

Presenting animals to the public and to judges at fairs can help boost the confidence of young 4-H members.

THE STRUCTURE OF 4-H

As a large organization, 4-H needs many people at various levels to keep things running smoothly. The organization has four basic levels. These are local, county, state, and national levels.

Individual clubs make up the local level. Local clubs must have at least five members, but the average is 24 members. A club elects youth officers and chooses its own programs. Officer positions include president, vice president, secretary, and treasurer. At least one adult leader oversees each club, and the leader may be supported by junior leaders. Junior leaders are youth in grades 7 through 12 who assist the adult leader and mentor younger 4-H students. Clubs may be based out of schools or communities. They must meet at least six times per year.

Local 4-H meetings may be held in places such as churches and classrooms.

A 4-H extension agent visits a classroom on National Youth Science Day to lead the group in a science experiment.

Each county has at least one 4-H extension agent who oversees its clubs. There can be several more agents depending on the county's population. If there is a big city with a lot of clubs, agents may be dedicated to just that city. The county funds the staff and operations.

At the national level, 4-H is operated by the US Department of Agriculture.

Above the county level is the state level, where the Cooperative Extension Service runs 4-H. This is a group of more than 100 public universities in states and on tribal reservations, each of which has a 4-H office and runs programs to educate youth. States fund these 4-H offices and programs.

The national level is the top level of the organization. The USDA's Cooperative State Research, Education, and Extension Service is home to the national headquarters for 4-H. Staff at this level identify key issues for youth across the country and help develop programs to address those issues.

In addition to government funding, nonprofit foundations provide financial support and help start programs for 4-H. The National 4-H Council is a nonprofit organization that raises funding for 4-H. It provides the organization with legal and communications services. It also helps create educational plans for 4-H. Additionally, state and county foundations may sometimes help provide funding and support programs at a state and local level.

In 2012, the National 4-H Council recognized former member Jennifer Nettles, *left*, a successful singer, with a Distinguished Alumni Medallion at its Legacy Awards event.

Students in the Cloverbud program may help their families show livestock at fairs.

4-H PROGRAMS

Programs give 4-H club members opportunities to complete hands-on projects while receiving guidance from adults. The organization has two main programs for students, based on age. The Cloverbud program is for ages five to eight, from kindergarten to grade 2. At this age, children are encouraged to develop skills such as the ability to work together. No competition is involved. Cloverbuds have the option to participate in day camps or short overnight camps. They might do arts and crafts, have a campfire to learn about fire safety, or learn about livestock. There are also after-school programs for Cloverbuds that provide fun educational activities focused on farming, nutrition, science, and more.

Cloverbuds do not have animal projects. However, some activities teach them how to handle animals. When Cloverbuds are interacting with animals directly, an adult or older teenager must be in control of the animal, no matter the size. This keeps the child and animal safe. Cloverbuds can learn about feeding, watering, and grooming animals. They can try hand milking dairy goats, training rabbits or other small pets, caring for and training dogs, and riding horses. They may also plant seeds and help them grow.

Caring for animals, such as rabbits, helps Cloverbuds learn skills they can use as they grow within 4-H.

CLOVER

Students ages eight to eighteen can participate in the CLOVER program. Students can choose from many project categories. These include traditional farming topics such as animals and crops, along with arts, health, civics, and environmental science. Project availability can vary by state based on local needs. For example, states with limited water resources have programs to educate students about water conservation in agriculture and other areas of life. If a student chooses an

Students interested in science may choose projects that involve doing experiments.

animal project, the student or members of the student's household must either lease or own the animals.

With livestock projects, a student can select one animal to raise. Project animals include beef cattle, dairy cattle, meat goats, dairy goats, llamas, alpacas, poultry, rabbits, sheep, and swine. Students must learn all about the type of animal they are raising. This includes the animal's breed, anatomy, health, and proper handling. They learn how to care for the animal by providing proper nutrition, committing to feeding and watering schedules, and grooming. Students learn about the behavior of the animal. They study the animal's reproductive cycle. For dairy animals, students may study milking. They learn how to read a pedigree, which is a record of an animal's descent. Students also study the ethics of raising livestock and practice marketing their animals.

The poultry category of birds includes chickens, turkeys, ducks, and geese.

Students train their animals to walk calmly using a piece of headgear called a halter.

During livestock projects, students are encouraged to be responsible for the daily care of their animals. Youth typically spend more than a year raising their animals. Many students have the goal of showing their cow, pig, or other animal at their county fair. Those who do well at the county fair can go on to show their animals at the state fair.

Some students choose a market project. This means raising animals to be sold at market, after which the animals will be harvested for food. Typically, at the end of the project, students bring their animals to a fair. There, judges weigh the animals to make sure they meet market weight. Then the animals are auctioned off.

Livestock auctions give farmers an opportunity to earn money after working hard to raise an animal.

The 4-H member gets money from the sale of the animal, but it can be an emotional goodbye. There is some debate about whether 4-H members, especially very young ones, should raise animals for market. However, children are not required to choose these projects. They have many other options. Even if they do pick animal projects, they do not have to participate in fairs where the animals are auctioned.

It may be challenging for 4-H members to say goodbye to an animal after developing a bond with it over time.

Animal-related activities are sometimes controversial when it comes to the very youngest 4-H members.

A 2010 study found that auctions are especially difficult for youth aged 13 and younger. When choosing a market project, they may not always truly understand what will happen to the animal. They may not predict how hard it will be to let the animal go when the time comes. The months that youth spend caring for and training their animals can build bonds similar to those between pets and owners.

For many 4-H families, it is important that youth learn the realities of raising livestock for food.

However, people also note the importance of not sheltering youth from the reality of where their food comes from. The process of raising market animals teaches youth about meat production and the importance of raising food animals ethically. It teaches them to value animals and not waste food.

OTHER ANIMAL PROJECTS

Youth in 4-H have other options for animal projects beyond raising livestock. Students can learn about safety around horses, horse care, training, and riding. They can compete in county and state horse shows. Riders can compete in roping, barrel racing, and other events. Youth can train an untrained horse. Those without access to horses can do projects such as creating educational exhibits or demonstrating knowledge using a mentor's horse.

4-H members learn important animal skills, such as how to safely wash their horses.

Students can do projects with dogs too. They learn about breeds, care, and training. They can compete in obedience, agility, and showmanship events. Obedience tests the dog and handler on the dog's ability to perform behaviors such as sit, down, stay, and come. In agility events, handlers guide their dogs through an obstacle course as quickly as possible. In showmanship competitions, youth learn how to groom and handle their dogs for evaluation against a breed standard. However, in 4-H, dogs do not need to be purebred to compete.

Members can also do projects with cats. They learn about breeds, handling, showmanship, and safe transportation. In showmanship competitions, judges evaluate the relationship

Young 4-H members compete in a dog showmanship event at the San Mateo County Fair in California.

People who want to show their cats in competitions must develop a strong bond with their pets.

between the cat and its handler. They may judge how well the handler keeps the cat under control and whether the cat and handler are relaxed. Other small pets can also be used for projects. These include rabbits, gerbils, birds, snakes, and fish.

Horticulture competitions may involve creating arrangements of plants or flowers.

PLANTS

Other common 4-H projects center around plants. Some students grow crops such as corn, learning about how the soil affects crop production. Others focus on horticulture. They grow flowers. They learn how to plant and grow a garden, how to fertilize it, and how to use various gardening tools. They get experience propagating flowers, which involves causing plants to reproduce. They also learn about different types of houseplants.

Another 4-H project is growing a vegetable, fruit, or herb garden. Youth plant, water, and fertilize the garden. They prune the plants and weed as needed. They learn how to identify beneficial insects and prevent pests and diseases.

Youth in 4-H planted a garden at a farm in Maine. The garden supplied local food pantries with fresh produce.

SUSTAINABILITY

4-H puts focus on sustainability and conservation in modern farming practices for both small and large farms. The practices of crop rotation, planting cover crops, site-specific nutrient management, and organic farming are necessary and often utilized in efforts to maintain a healthy environment and balance what is invested and harvested.

Farmers work to safely use chemicals to control pests and weeds to maximize yields.

Large-scale farms may include multiple vast buildings where animals are raised.

4-H is dedicated to teaching the next generation of farmers so that they can develop more sustainable approaches to agriculture. 4-H members are encouraged to explore topics related to sustainability solutions. Students have completed more than one million environmental projects.

The Altria corporation is involved in the tobacco growing industry. It is among the largest corporate supporters of 4-H.

Large-scale agricultural companies are also called big ag. They are among the leading financial supporters of 4-H. 4-H educates students about how large-scale farming works.

The huge harvests of big ag are necessary to feed the world's growing population. Big ag companies aren't 4-H's only major donors. Other foundations that emphasize health and the environment also provide funding for 4-H. 4-H incorporates these topics in its programs. Many local extension agents at the county level encourage clubs to think about sustainable practices.

Farmers can take advantage of technology to improve the sustainability of their farms.

Droughts, or extended periods without rainfall, can have a severe impact on farmers. Learning about water conservation can help people manage these challenges.

There are many opportunities for 4-H members to do projects and participate in programs that emphasize sustainability. For example, students can study water conservation in agriculture. Oklahoma 4-H holds an annual 4-H Water Fair in elementary and middle schools. It teaches students about keeping water sources healthy and using water sustainably. Students can also choose to complete an environmental science project, which involves learning about soil erosion, climate change, and environmental challenges.

In addition, 70,000 4-H students have participated in a program called the 4-H Ag Innovators Experience. This program covers the importance of taking care of the environment in an agricultural setting. Students learn about how agriculture affects insect populations. They also learn about cutting-edge practices and tools that help farms operate more sustainably.

A 4-H team from Minnesota gives a presentation about using drones to protect livestock from predators.

Each year has a different theme. In 2020, the theme was the Water Connects Us All Challenge. Participants learned about how ecosystems can improve or worsen water quality. Krish Nangia, a 4-H member in Illinois, noted, "Many of us take water, a precious resource, for granted, so it is extremely important for youth to understand agriculture topics, such as the Water Connects Us All Challenge, because these problems cannot be resolved without working together as a team." In 2021, the theme was the Curbing Our Carbon Appetite Challenge. Participants explored how the agricultural industry could reduce carbon emissions. The 2023 theme was the Aerial Ag Challenge. Participants learned about

Tractors that run on batteries rather than fossil fuels can help farmers reduce their carbon emissions.

In addition to its work on agricultural chemicals and seeds, Bayer is a major pharmaceutical company.

how drones and precision agriculture help make farming more efficient.

The Ag Innovators Experience is run through a collaboration between 4-H and the company Bayer. Bayer is a German company with locations in the United States. It focuses on researching crops and developing seeds. Each year, several thousand students participate in the program.

OTHER PROJECTS

The 4-H organization offers many other agricultural projects. Students can learn about tractors and farm equipment. Through these projects, they can explore the history of tractors and equipment, as well as how this machinery is designed and operated. They might learn how to drive the equipment and perform maintenance to keep it running smoothly. Club members study the safety guidelines for using farm equipment. Some students even restore a tractor or machine as part of their project. Similarly, students might learn about small engines, how they work, and

A 4-H member from Pennsylvania restored a Farmall tractor from 1937 to show at a county fair.

Water pollution of all kinds can have a negative impact on agriculture.

how to repair them. They may study different kinds of fuels and their uses.

Students can also do projects related to bodies of water and wetlands. They can learn about how to use water sustainably. They may study how agriculture and urban development can pollute waters. Students can learn how to minimize this pollution and conserve water resources.

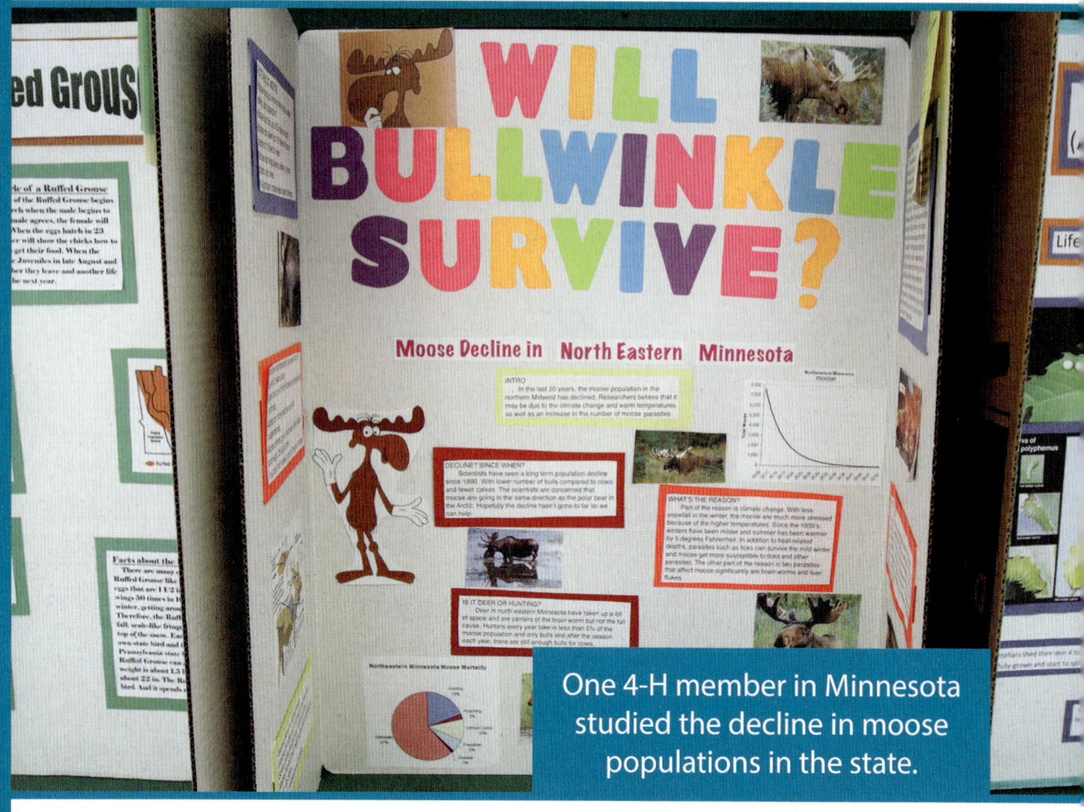

One 4-H member in Minnesota studied the decline in moose populations in the state.

Beyond agriculture, there are many other categories of projects. These include nutrition, computers, engineering, veterinary science, and robotics. These fields all have potential overlap with agriculture. People in 4-H can also create their own projects. They typically start by picking a topic that interests them.

Some state 4-H agencies have forms that can help students develop a project. This form might have students research their topic before starting. Then they can select learning experiences, such as attending a workshop or demonstration related to the topic or organizing a club activity based on the project. They must also demonstrate leadership. Participants may do this by helping other club members with their projects or by inviting an expert to speak to the club about the topic. Students may give presentations at the end of their projects.

A 4-H student in Florida delivers a presentation on cooking.

NATIONAL 4-H CONFERENCE

Each year in the spring, a few 4-H students from each state have the chance to attend the National 4-H Conference. Youth interested in attending the conference must be between 15 and 19 years old, although some states require delegates to be older than 16. They typically have to fill out an application with their state 4-H department. The application might include essay questions. It may also ask for a list of the student's 4-H accomplishments. State 4-H departments select a certain number of students to send as delegates to the conference. Students may not be allowed to apply if they have already attended the conference in a prior year.

The secretary of the USDA, Tom Vilsack, addressed delegates at the National 4-H Conference in 2011.

4-H members met with Maine senator Angus King while visiting Washington, DC, for the National 4-H Conference.

At this conference, delegates meet with each other to discuss key issues and develop potential solutions. Then they share these important issues and strategies with US government officials. When a state's delegates return home, they work to put a plan into action for one of the issues discussed. Delegates typically have to pay for a portion of the trip, but scholarships cover the rest.

Arkansas 4-H sent more than three dozen delegates to the 2021 National 4-H Congress.

NATIONAL 4-H CONGRESS

Another important event on the 4-H calendar is the National 4-H Congress. This gathering is held yearly in November. States select applicants to send as delegates to the five-day event. The delegates participate in educational workshops, listen to speakers, and get to know 4-H members and business professionals from other states.

At the 2023 congress, participants learned from speakers such as Dionne Toombs, the associate director for programs at the National Institute of Food and Agriculture. This agency provides funding for education, research, and extension programs related to agriculture. Another speaker was Chris Boleman, the president and CEO of the Houston Livestock Show and Rodeo. He was formerly Texas 4-H's state leader.

One workshop discussed skills for connecting with people. This helps students with college and job interviews, as well as with personal relationships. Another workshop instructed participants on how to provide service to others and how to learn from service. Other workshops centered around mental health.

Topics of discussion at the National 4-H Congress go beyond traditional farming subjects and might include subjects such as social media skills.

Students could also enjoy activities such as a dance and a tour of Atlanta, Georgia. This is where the conference took place. They could explore different locations throughout the city.

At the 2022 congress, students had the chance to tour the Georgia Aquarium and the College Football Hall of Fame, among other local highlights. As with the National 4-H Conference, delegates typically pay for part of the trip, while the rest is covered by scholarships.

Awards and recognition are common parts of many 4-H gatherings.

AWARDS

In addition to participating in programs, 4-H members can receive awards for their hard work. These awards have certain criteria, such as having demonstrated a certain character trait or being a certain age. Students in the University of California 4-H program can receive a Golden Clover Award. There are many categories in this award, including one for personal growth, one for beekeeping, and one for innovative ideas. Recipients get a medallion, a pin, and a small cash prize.

4-H members can win a variety of medals, ribbons, and plaques for outstanding achievements.

Often, states have an award to recognize the top club members in the state. Texas's highest award is the Gold Star. Students who are in grade 9 or higher and have been part of 4-H for three years are eligible for this award. They must have participated in activities such as 4-H camps, leadership experiences, and competitive events. Recipients are given a pin. A 4-H member can receive this award only once.

Certain programs also give out awards. The Youth in Action program provides training in using different kinds of media, giving interviews, and telling stories. Every year, the organization selects four award winners from the program to receive a $5,000 college scholarship. The winners have the opportunity to travel for free while acting as a national spokesperson for the organization.

Patches and ribbons may become treasured symbols of a person's time in 4-H.

4-H INFLUENCE

Because 4-H is so large, it has influenced the lives of many youth, as well as communities and the agricultural industry. On an individual level, a 2019 study found that 4-H helps youth become successful adults. According to that study, 84 percent of 4-H alumni were satisfied with their lives. This was 14 percentage points higher than those who were not members of 4-H. Alumni were also more likely than nonparticipants to be satisfied with their community connections, mental and emotional health, jobs, and other aspects of their lives.

One reason for these results is that 4-H helps prepare youth for careers. It also helps them develop life skills that can help

Some 4-H members give public presentations to encourage young people to join 4-H.

Working on 4-H projects can help students develop public speaking skills that are useful for jobs in any industry.

them outside of their careers. One such skill is public speaking. 4-H students often give presentations to their local clubs about what they are learning through their projects. They must learn how to research a topic, organize the information, present that information clearly, and create visual aids such as graphs to use during their presentations. Students may also have opportunities to present to larger audiences, such as when delegates at the National 4-H Conference speak to large groups of peers and US government officials.

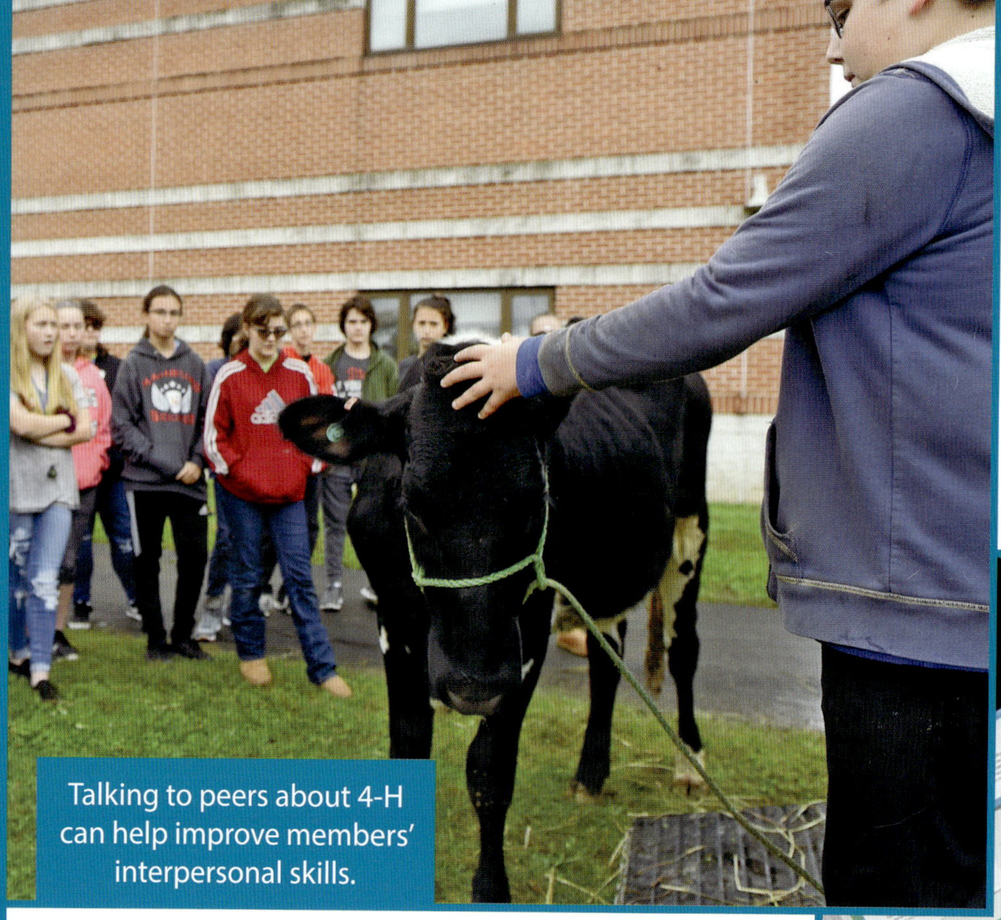

Talking to peers about 4-H can help improve members' interpersonal skills.

These same skills help students prepare for college. In addition, people who were in 4-H credit the organization with helping them develop interpersonal skills. Being part of clubs and attending camps where they lived with other people for a few days helped them form good relationships with roommates and classmates. Students also note how 4-H helped teach them about time management and gave them the ability to meet deadlines, which are useful in college and many other areas of life.

The organization can also help students handle the financial demands of college. The organization offers scholarships for 4-H alumni. These scholarships have various criteria, including exemplary leadership, completion of major projects, and receiving certain 4-H awards. Some are available only to alumni who are enrolled in an agricultural degree program.

Successfully completing and presenting projects can put 4-H members in the running for valuable scholarships.

Animal and plant projects help prepare youth for careers in agriculture. Projects can help youth discover what type of livestock or crops they want to farm. These projects also introduce them to the full process of growing crops or raising livestock. Students can participate in the entire process, from preparing the soil for planting to selling the crop. They can raise

Many 4-H members gain hands-on experience with raising animals.

Raising animals requires hard work and perseverance, qualities that can be applied to many other parts of life.

a baby animal, present it to judges, and then sell it at auction. Everything students learn through the process, such as how to prevent pests or what to feed a certain animal, can help them as they enter a career in agriculture.

Students say that working on 4-H projects helped them learn the value of hard work. They learned to persevere through struggles and overcome adversity. This gives them the confidence to set goals and meet challenges as adults.

Cleaning up litter is one way that 4-H members give back to their communities.

The 4-H organization provides students with many volunteer opportunities. Clubs may organize activities such as picking up trash along roadsides or volunteering at food pantries. Through volunteering, youth learn about the needs of their communities. They can help address these needs through volunteer opportunities. They can also go beyond that and look for new ways to help.

COMMUNITY SUPPORT

As they learn and grow on a personal level, 4-H members are encouraged to give back to their communities. This benefits communities by helping people who are not part of 4-H thrive. For example, Pearl Daskam and Addy Battel from Michigan learned that people in their community were facing food insecurity. Many did not have access to high-quality protein sources. The two 4-H students began raising chickens to donate to their local food pantry.

Members can use the agricultural skills they learn in 4-H to help their communities.

Hunter Williams of Florida similarly learned about food insecurity. In 2020, Williams was 17 years old. The COVID-19 pandemic caused a lot of disruption to supply chains, including those for food products. Schools and restaurants were forced to close to prevent the spread of the virus. Although people were eating mainly at home, sales from grocery stores did not increase enough to compensate for the loss of school and restaurant buyers. As a result, many farmers had a surplus of food. They donated some to food shelves, but the food shelves had a limited number of refrigerators and freezers. In addition, harvesting crops and transporting them when people were not

The COVID-19 pandemic caused significant challenges and uncertainty for farmers across the country.

Selling boxes of produce directly from farmers is a practice known as community supported agriculture.

buying them was costly. Some farmers ended up dumping milk or plowing crops back into the fields.

Williams decided to help both farmers and people facing food insecurity. He recruited family and friends to help buy boxes of produce from farmers. Most farmers sold just one type of produce, such as tomatoes, blueberries, onions, squash, or kale. After buying bulk produce from several farmers, Williams would pack boxes with some of each type. He then sold the assorted produce boxes to people in Florida. As a result of his work, farmers continued to get paid for some of their harvest, and people who lived in areas without access to a variety of fruits and vegetables could buy these nutritious foods.

Repairing county fairgrounds benefits not only 4-H clubs but also the surrounding community.

HELPING COUNTY FAIRGROUNDS

Youth in 4-H often present their projects at county fairs. Because of their close ties with county fairgrounds, some clubs give back by helping with repairs. In 2023, two clubs in Ohio helped improve the Wood County Fairgrounds. Duke's Mixture 4-H Club painted a popular food vendor stand. The All Tacked Up 4-H Club teamed up with adult volunteers to repair the photography area at the horse arena. Members tore down old wooden paneling and put up new metal siding. They installed a sign. They also did landscaping, laying down mulch and bringing in potted plants for decoration. Their improvements gave riders a more attractive spot to take photographs with their horses.

Sometimes entire clubs work on fairground improvements, but other times individual 4-H members choose a fairground task as their project. In Pennsylvania, Caleb Miller installed cattle gates on a barn at the Elizabethtown Fairgrounds. Damian Brown rebuilt a storage closet at Montour-DeLong Community Fairgrounds. Both received Diamond Clover Awards, which is Pennsylvania 4-H's highest level of achievement. Improvements at fairgrounds can make buildings look nicer for visitors and improve public safety.

Clubs also use fairs to educate younger children about agriculture. The Simply Stock 4-H Club in Ohio created a coloring book containing pictures of livestock along with facts about the animals. Members ran the coloring stations, handing out crayons and books to children.

The Iowa State Fair has high-quality facilities, but many smaller venues are in need of repair.

Some fairground improvement projects take a long time. Morgan Deiter of the 4-H Horse and Pony Club renovated a horse arena at the Perry County Fairgrounds in Pennsylvania. Working alongside family and friends, she spent 155 hours over two years on her project. The arena was more than 20 years old, and it was the only safe place for many local riders to practice.

A well-maintained horse arena is safer for horses and riders.

Renovating a horse arena takes a lot of time and money. To do this type of project, 4-H members may need to find funding or help from professionals.

Deiter had to raise money for the project, holding fundraisers and contacting local businesses for donations. During the COVID-19 pandemic in 2020, the cost of materials for the project more than tripled from the estimates she had originally received. So she had to work hard to get enough funding. Deiter contacted more than 180 businesses across the country.

Once she had the materials, she and her team got to work. The old fence posts around the arena were starting to rot, so she removed them and replaced them with new ones. Some gates were becoming difficult to open and close, which could be a safety hazard if a rider needed to leave the arena in an emergency. Deiter purchased and installed new gates, and she also bought and spread new dirt in the arena.

Therapy involving horses is also known as hippotherapy, from the Greek word for "horse."

OTHER COMMUNITY IMPROVEMENTS

Beyond fairgrounds, club members make improvements in other parts of their communities. In 2023, Katherine Fogel received a Diamond Clover Award for her project to make a sensory trail for the TaKE Center. This Pennsylvania center uses horses to help provide physical therapy to people with physical and cognitive challenges. On the sensory trail, clients ride their horses through a curtain of suspended pool noodles, which part around the rider's head. On another part of the trail, riders aim and toss balls into painted tires. They also play tic-tac-toe on horseback, flipping signs to reveal an *X* or an *O*.

Clubs and individual members can also help schools and neighborhoods. They might build raised garden beds for schools. The schools can use these garden beds to give students hands-on experience growing crops and other plants. 4-H members might also build community gardens for neighborhoods. Community gardens provide space for people who don't have their own gardens. They can grow their own food rather than buying it from grocery stores.

There are about 29,000 community gardens in the 100 largest US cities.

Another type of garden a 4-H club might make is a pollinator garden. Pollinator gardens provide food for pollinators such as bees and butterflies. These insects travel from flower to flower, eating nectar and pollen. They help spread pollen from one flower to another, which is important for helping plants reproduce. Pollinator gardens help these important insect populations grow. This in turn helps agriculture, because many crops, such as apples, almonds, grapes, and tomatoes, require pollination to grow.

In South Carolina, 4-H students planned and planted a pollinator garden in the Conestee Nature Preserve. The students also helped care for the garden after it opened.

Drawing pollinators to an area helps promote a healthy ecosystem and also benefits agriculture.

A 4-H project inspired a Minnesota teen to build a pollinator garden at her home.

The garden was designed to help visitors learn about pollinators and their importance in nature.

FUNDRAISING

Some clubs hold fundraisers for nonprofit organizations. In Texas, club members in Liberty Hill held a bake sale. They raised $600, which they used to buy 75 coats to donate to Operation Liberty Hill. This organization provides free food, clothing, and household items to community members in need.

Sheep, which are easier to raise than larger livestock such as cattle, are a popular choice for young 4-H members.

Youth in 4-H often help their communities. But sometimes communities help the youth. Nine-year-old Idaho 4-H member Makenzie Peters was raising a sheep, Rose, to show in 2023. That summer, doctors discovered a mass on the girl's brain. She had two brain surgeries. Her friend, Dash Jones, was raising his own 4-H sheep at the time and cared for Rose while Peters recovered. He made sure Rose was ready for the Gem/Boise County Fair.

The day before the fair, Peters's doctor gave her permission to go to the fair and show Rose. She did, and her whole 4-H club showed up to support her. Later, when her sheep was up for auction, people began bidding on Rose. Then they began pledging add-on bids, and altogether the auction raised more than $27,000 to help Peters's family pay for ongoing medical expenses.

4-H members may be involved in livestock auctions. The money from auctions is sometimes used to support the community.

OTHER INFLUENCE

4-H members influence their communities in an educational setting. They conduct research and give presentations to adults and students to educate them about various aspects of agriculture. For example, they may teach a class for younger students about the kinds of crops and livestock that are raised locally. They may teach drivers and horse riders how to share the road safely.

Opportunities for club members to educate the public aren't limited to local audiences. Using video-call technology, clubs can bring the latest agricultural information to people around the globe. Wyatt Nikodym and other club members in Oklahoma used Zoom to present 4-H programming about water pollution and conservation to 4-H leaders in the Republic of the Congo.

In addition to showing their animals, 4-H members use fairs to help educate the public about agriculture.

Rain gardens have many benefits, including preventing erosion and attracting pollinators.

One topic the club members covered was how to use rain gardens. These gardens are made in a depressed, or lower, spot of land designed to hold runoff water from roofs, driveways, and other human structures that don't absorb water. Eventually, the water in the rain garden seeps into the ground. Plants in the rain garden help filter out pollution and allow more water to soak into the soil than regular lawns do.

Rain gardens are dry most of the time, filling with water only after a rainfall. They are especially useful in urban areas, where green spaces have been largely replaced by concrete and other materials that water cannot penetrate. During the presentation, students taught the leaders how to make a rain garden and discussed ideal locations for these types of gardens.

Youth can also use their own areas of expertise to help adults. Lucy Teuteberg, a 4-H member in Washington State, helps teach adults how to use technology. She teaches them how to set up computers so they can work remotely, and she also explains how to avoid online scams. Other topics include teaching people how to identify which websites are safe and reputable, as well as helping people without reliable internet connections get access to important resources. Teuteberg's work has benefited not only adults but also herself. Her mother noted that Teuteberg had become more confident and eager to help others as a result of the program.

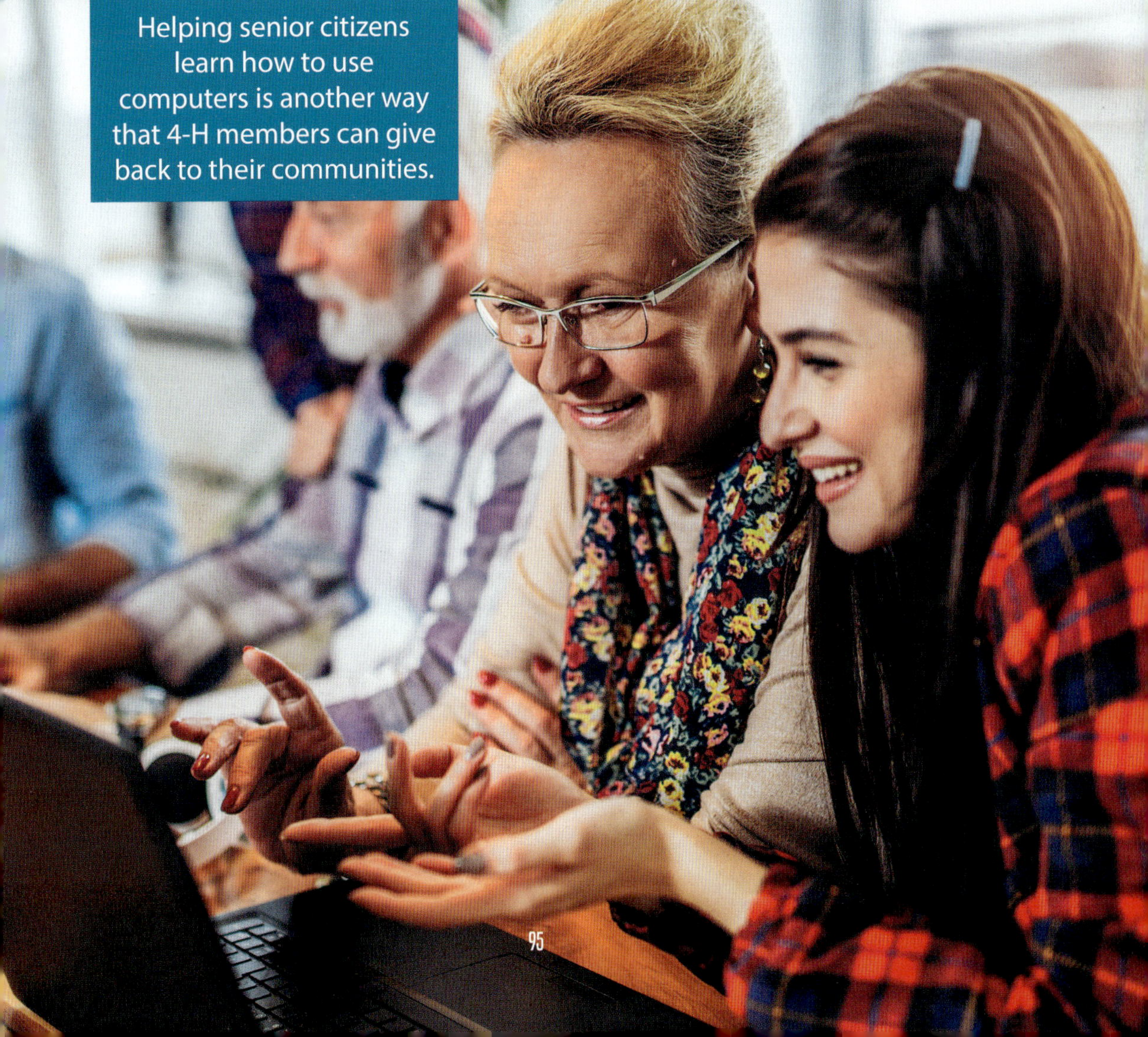

Helping senior citizens learn how to use computers is another way that 4-H members can give back to their communities.

JOINING 4-H

The 4-H organization provides youth with many opportunities for growth and development. People who are interested in joining a club can use the Find Your Local 4-H feature on the 4-H website to find clubs near them. Some clubs focus on certain areas of interest, such as agriculture or robotics. Students may want to find a club that emphasizes their own specific interests. Other clubs have more general topics but are more conveniently located. Once students know which club they would like to join, their parents or guardians can contact the county extension office to enroll the students in that club.

There is no national enrollment fee. However, some states, counties, or individual clubs may charge a club participation fee. Some projects and other experiences, such as camps, also cost money. However, people may be able to receive financial aid if needed.

Millions of young people have participated in 4-H since the organization was founded.

Members have been learning and living by the 4-H pledge for about a century.

THE HISTORY OF FFA

In the early 1900s, young people in the United States were losing interest in farming. Boys whose parents farmed were leaving their family farms to pursue other careers. But in 1925, four agricultural educators at the Virginia Polytechnic Institute's Agricultural Education Department looked for a way to keep more boys interested in agricultural careers. These educators were Walter S. Newman, Edmund C. Magill, Harry Sanders, and Henry Groseclose.

Newman envisioned a program that would help boys develop leadership skills and encourage them to take pride in being farm boys. Groseclose wrote a constitution and bylaws for the organization. It was named the Future Farmers of Virginia. Launched in 1926, this statewide organization oversaw local chapters, which were made for boys who were in high school agriculture classes. It started a newsletter to let chapters across the state share news and information. A naming contest was held for the newsletter, and the winning name was *Chapter Chats*.

Walter S. Newman later served as the president of Virginia Polytechnic Institute from 1947 until 1962.

Henry Groseclose was the first executive secretary of Future Farmers of America, serving from 1928 to 1930.

Similar clubs formed in other states at this time. Some taught boys how to grow soybeans. Others taught girls how to grow tomatoes. In 1927, the New Farmers of Virginia formed. Agricultural educators G. W. Owens and J. R. Thomas, along with federal agricultural education official H. O. Sargent, started the organization. It was similar to the Future Farmers of Virginia, but it was for Black students.

At the time, Virginia's schools were segregated. Black students attended different schools than

H. O. Sargent began teaching students in Black schools about agriculture in 1917.

Young Black farmers faced poverty and segregation. The New Farmers of Virginia provided important support.

white students. The Future Farmers of Virginia operated in white schools while the New Farmers of Virginia operated in Black schools. Over time, organizations similar to the New Farmers of Virginia started in other states.

NATIONAL ORGANIZATIONS

Male students from 18 states came together at the 1928 National Livestock Judging Contests, which were held in Kansas City, Missouri. These 33 students formed the Future Farmers of America (FFA). The national organization would be modeled after the Future Farmers of Virginia. It would give farm boys leadership training.

After forming the organization, the students elected Leslie Applegate as the first national president. Applegate was a student from New Jersey. The students set membership dues at

A cattle judging contest was among the events at the first FFA meeting.

10 cents per year. This gathering became the first National FFA Convention, which has since been held yearly.

By 1929, there were approximately 30,000 FFA members in 35 states. The organization continued to develop. Its official colors became national blue and corn gold. In that year, the organization also gave out its first Star Farmer of America award, later renamed the American Star Farmer. This award honors members who demonstrate exceptional achievement and receive excellent grades. Carlton Patton of Arkansas was the first recipient of the Star Farmer of America award.

1930s

In 1930, FFA members adopted a creed. Agricultural educator Erwin Milton Tiffany wrote the creed as he was preparing for the organization's third national convention. The creed speaks of FFA's values, including being a responsible citizen, demonstrating leadership, and being a hard worker. It consists of five "I believe" statements that cover a hope for a good future in agriculture; the joys and challenges of farming; the importance of respect, leadership, and hard work; and the ability of individuals to influence the agricultural community. The organization later made revisions to the text at the 38th and 63rd annual conventions, creating the version of the creed used today.

Erwin Milton Tiffany taught students about agriculture at the University of Wisconsin.

Photos from FFA events in the 1930s demonstrate the gender restrictions of the group's early history.

At the same national convention in 1930, FFA delegates officially limited membership to boys. Girls were not permitted to become FFA members. Over the next few decades, some chapters did allow girls to participate in meetings and competitions at the local or state levels. The girls sometimes had to use their initials to hide their gender. But they were not allowed full FFA membership. Girls interested in agriculture did not have access to the national events and developmental opportunities that boys did.

In 1933, FFA adopted its iconic blue jacket. J. H. "Gus" Lintner was the adviser of the Fredericktown, Ohio, FFA chapter. He saw a blue corduroy jacket in a store and asked the maker to stitch the chapter's name on the back. The chapter members wore the jackets at the National FFA Convention that year. Other FFA members at the convention liked the jackets and adopted them as the official dress of FFA. Over the decades, other items of clothing and accessories would be added to the official dress, and the jacket was later modified.

The official dress of FFA includes the famous blue jacket, black pants or a skirt, a white shirt, and an FFA tie or scarf.

NFA members received instruction on many different farm tasks, including tractor repair.

In 1935, FFA reached more than 100,000 members. FFA did not officially exclude Black students, but because it was based out of segregated schools, Black students were largely excluded. The same year, the various state organizations for Black students joined to form the New Farmers of America (NFA). It operated much like FFA and ran many of the same programs. As with FFA, only boys could be members.

A group of NFA officers helped steer the overall direction of the organization.

The NFA national headquarters was at North Carolina A&T State University. One of the founding members of the NFA was S. B. Simmons. He had originally founded the North Carolina Association of the NFA. He later played a role at the national level of the NFA as the national executive secretary and the executive treasurer.

Like FFA, the NFA had its own creed. It followed a similar format, listing six "I believe" statements. The statements included that a farm boy's work would prosper the more he learned, that he would find a meaningful life in producing better crops and livestock and improving his home, and that it was important to develop leadership skills and use them in the community, government, and other areas of life. It also voiced the importance of helping others, working with others, and developing one's responsibility and talents.

The NFA creed emphasized hard work, service to the community, and self-improvement.

Booker T. Washington gave advice to President Theodore Roosevelt and President William Taft.

The NFA had several unique events too. Members celebrated National NFA Day on April 5. This was the same day as Booker T. Washington's birthday. Washington was born into slavery in 1856, but he was freed after the American

Civil War (1861–1865). Because his family lived in poverty, he began working at nine years old, so he was not able to receive traditional schooling for a while. Eventually, he found a job as a janitor at a school, which allowed him to receive an education there. In 1881, Washington founded the Tuskegee Normal and Industrial Institute, which provided Black Americans with a path to self-sufficiency by teaching them agricultural skills and other manual trades.

Eventually, National NFA Day turned into National NFA Week, which included presentations, banquets, and the crowning of Miss NFA. Like in FFA, girls could not be NFA members. But they could help promote NFA chapters as Sweethearts. They could compete for the title of Miss NFA at the chapter, district, and state levels. The winners received Miss NFA jackets, which were black with gold stitching.

An NFA exhibit at the 1939 World's Poultry Congress in Cleveland, Ohio, helped introduce the organization to new people.

1940s

The United States entered World War II (1939–1945) in December 1941. The nation dramatically increased its production of military equipment. Between 1942 and 1945, the country built approximately two million army trucks, 86,000 tanks, 297,000 aircraft, and 17 aircraft carriers. In order to produce the volume of vehicles and supplies needed for the war, many materials, factories, and companies that would have been dedicated to consumer goods were repurposed for war production. For example, car manufacturers made more than three million cars for public sale in 1941. But between

Factories making tanks and planes required massive amounts of raw materials during World War II.

December 1941 and September 1945, when the war ended, the nation made just 139 cars in total. The car manufacturers were instead making aircraft, trucks, and tanks.

This dramatic increase in production meant materials were stretched thin. The government started the Salvage for Victory campaign. It encouraged the public to collect material that could be used for the war effort.

Many Americans, including FFA members, contributed to the Salvage for Victory campaign.

Members of FFA joined this campaign. They collected scrap metal, rubber tires, and more from old, broken farm equipment in junk piles and ditches. Some farm equipment companies, including International Harvester, offered cash prizes to the clubs that collected the most scrap metal. In addition, some students dropped out of school and FFA in order to volunteer to fight in the war.

FFA was one of many organizations that helped raise money for the war effort during World War II.

Even though war disrupted many areas of life, the National FFA Convention continued to be held yearly. However, it was much smaller, with only delegates and award winners in attendance. FFA also experienced new developments during this time. The National FFA Foundation started in 1944 to help raise money for FFA's programs. And membership continued to rise. By 1948, there were approximately 250,000 FFA members.

In 1949, FFA debuted its white Sweetheart jacket. Because female students could not be full FFA members, they could not wear FFA's blue corduroy jackets. But girls involved in FFA as Chapter Sweethearts could now wear the Sweetheart jacket. Sweethearts were allowed to help as hostesses at FFA activities.

Girls were crowned as state Sweethearts at state-level FFA conferences.

1950s

The first issue of the *National Future Farmer* magazine was published in the fall of 1952. This official FFA magazine included information about raising and showing cattle, presenting awards, and the development of Louisiana's FFA dairy cattle program. The magazine was later renamed *FFA New Horizons*.

In 1959, FFA established its headquarters in Alexandria, Virginia. Since 1939, the organization had owned a portion

A 4-H member, *right*, gave a bread-baking demonstration to two FFA members at a California event in 1954.

At a 1965 ceremony, NFA president Adolphus Pinson, *right*, exchanged his NFA jacket for a new FFA jacket.

of land there that had previously been part of George Washington's estate. FFA had been using it as a camp location before building its headquarters there.

1960s

FFA reached a milestone in 1964, having sold one million FFA jackets by that year. That same year, the Civil Rights Act of 1964 made segregation and other forms of discrimination illegal. As a result, the NFA and FFA merged in 1965, retaining the FFA name. At the time of the merger, the NFA had 52,000 members who were transitioned to FFA.

In the end, the NFA lost many of the things that had set the organization apart, from its name to its awards and leadership. FFA didn't make any seats on its board of directors available to former NFA leaders, limiting the influence Black leaders had on the national organization. In addition, when schools and chapters merged, Black teachers often lost their jobs to white teachers. Because of the limited integration of Black leadership in FFA, morale began to drop in many Black students.

Some Black students saw success in their integrated chapters. Horace Hodge, who was in FFA from 1969 to 1973, ran for office in his chapter. He ran for the position of reporter, but his chapter appointed him president. However, other Black students were not elected to positions they had been striving for because of the larger number of white voters than Black voters. Alvin Larke was preparing to become an NFA national officer when the merger happened. He never got that chance, and it would be many years before a Black student received that position.

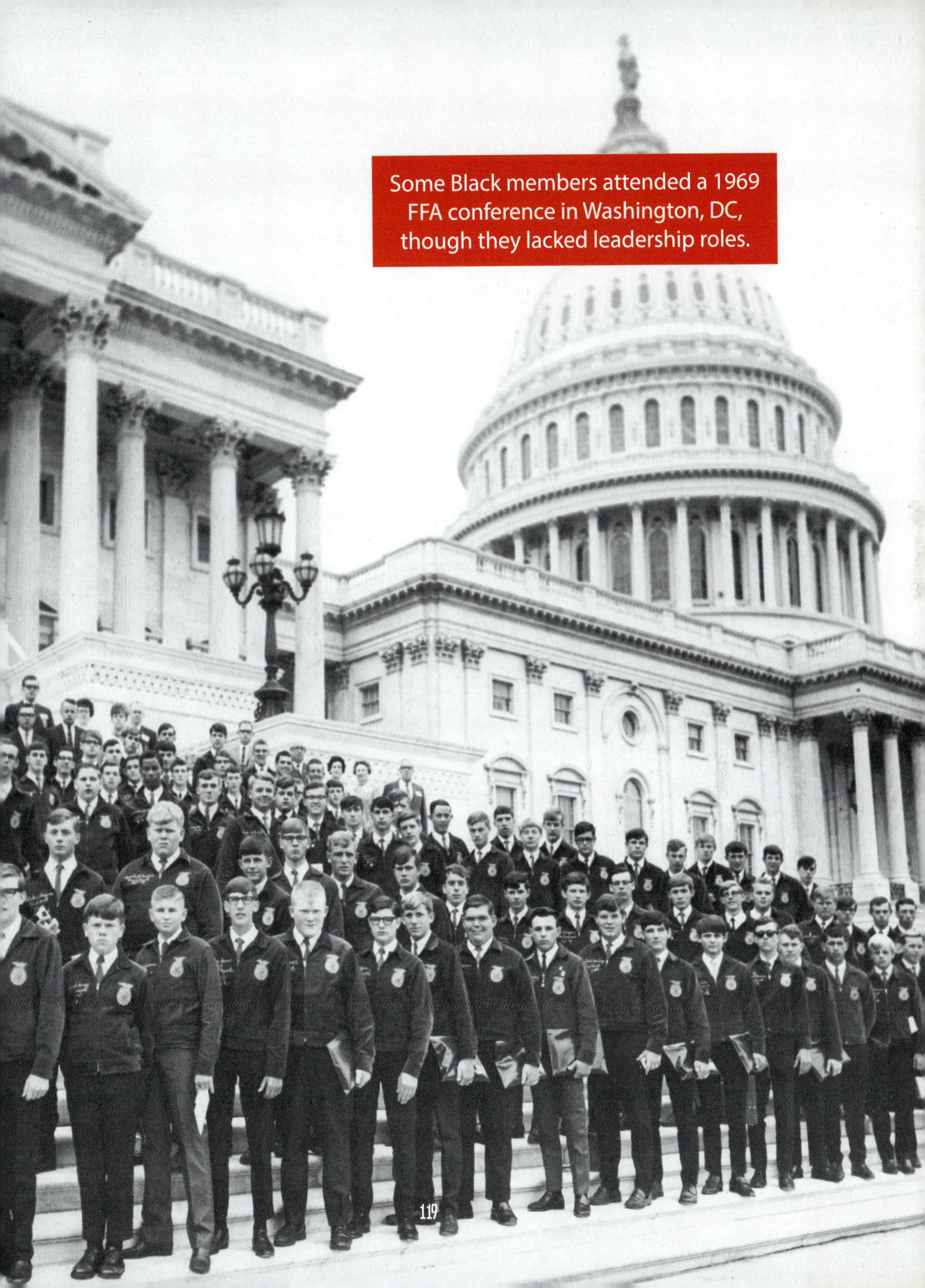

Some Black members attended a 1969 FFA conference in Washington, DC, though they lacked leadership roles.

In 1965, 52,000 Black students became part of FFA, which had a total enrollment of 450,000. But desegregation had unintended consequences. Black students had less representation in the new organization than they had in their former one. In 2022, there were 47,000 Black students in FFA, even though FFA had grown to more than 850,000 members.

In 1969, another demographic was accepted into FFA. An amendment to FFA's constitution, which passed by just two votes, gave girls and young women the ability to become full FFA members. They could hold office and compete at regional

Florida NFA members met in Tallahassee for a final State Convention before the merger with FFA.

From 1969 into the 1970s, female students were able to get involved in more of FFA's programs.

and national events. The FFA's official dress code was modified too. At the recommendation of an all-girls committee, female FFA members were required to wear skirts to FFA events.

Fred McClure met with Vice President Gerald R. Ford in 1974.

1970s–1980s

The next two decades featured many firsts for the organization. In 1970, the first female students were allowed full membership. Anita Decker of New York and Patricia Krowicki of New Jersey became the first young women to be delegates at the National FFA Convention. In 1973, Fred McClure of Texas became the first Black student elected to an FFA national office. He was appointed the western region vice president.

The 1980s saw more FFA firsts. In 1982, Jan Eberly of California was elected the first female national FFA president. Then in 1988, the organization changed its name from Future Farmers of America to the National FFA Organization. This change was prompted by the fact that membership had expanded to include people who were going into non-farming careers, though they still had some tie to agriculture. The new name was meant to encompass all students. That same year, membership opened to students in seventh and eighth grade.

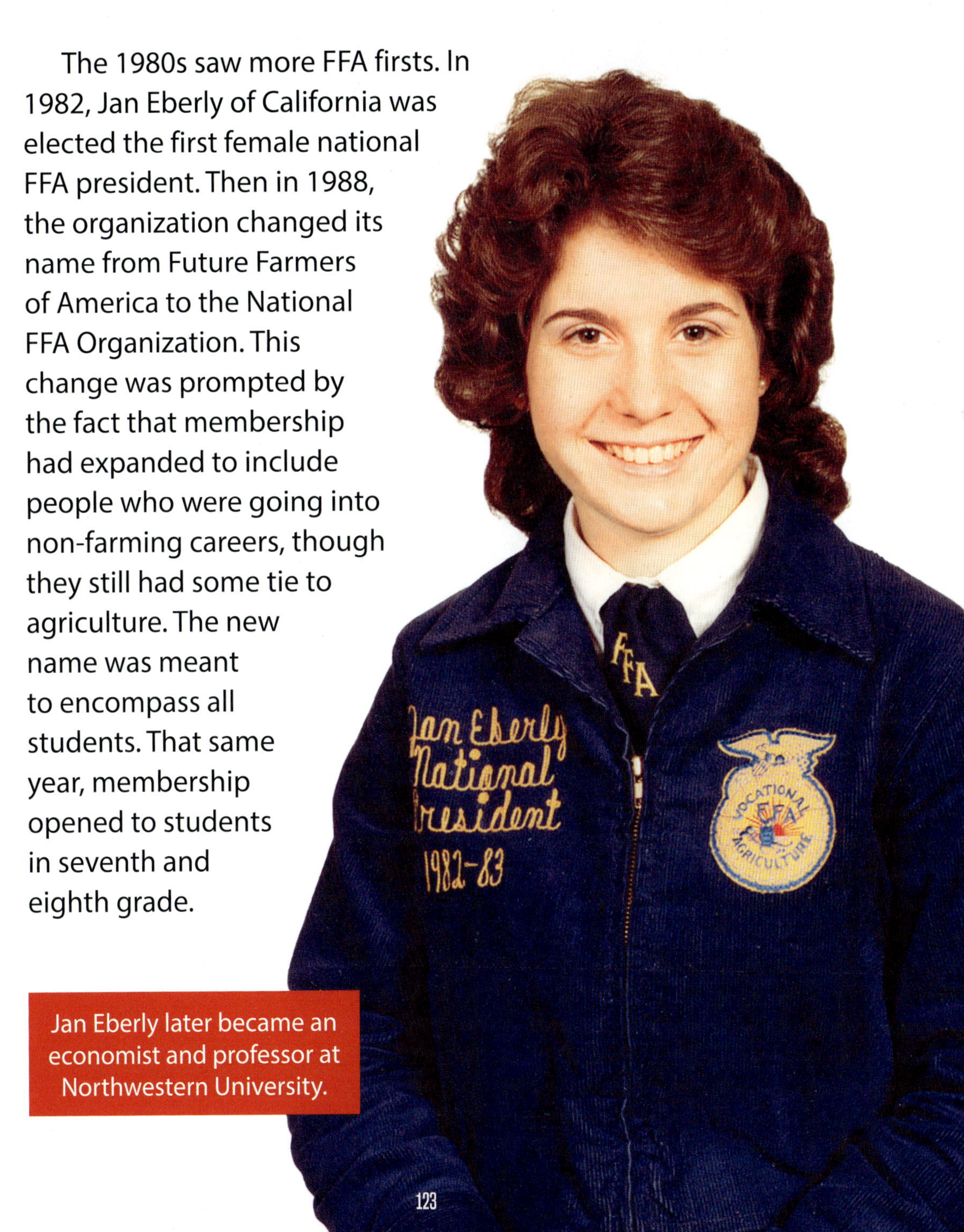

Jan Eberly later became an economist and professor at Northwestern University.

1990s–2000s

In 1994, Corey Flournoy of Illinois became the first Black student and the first student from an urban area to be elected national president of FFA. In 1999, the National FFA Convention location moved from Kansas City to Louisville, Kentucky, for the first time.

Karlene Lindow of Wisconsin became the first female member to be named American Star Farmer in 2002. She received this honor for her excellent work raising hogs.

Corey Flournoy used what he learned in FFA to become a successful business leader, returning to oversee equity, diversity, and inclusion in 2023.

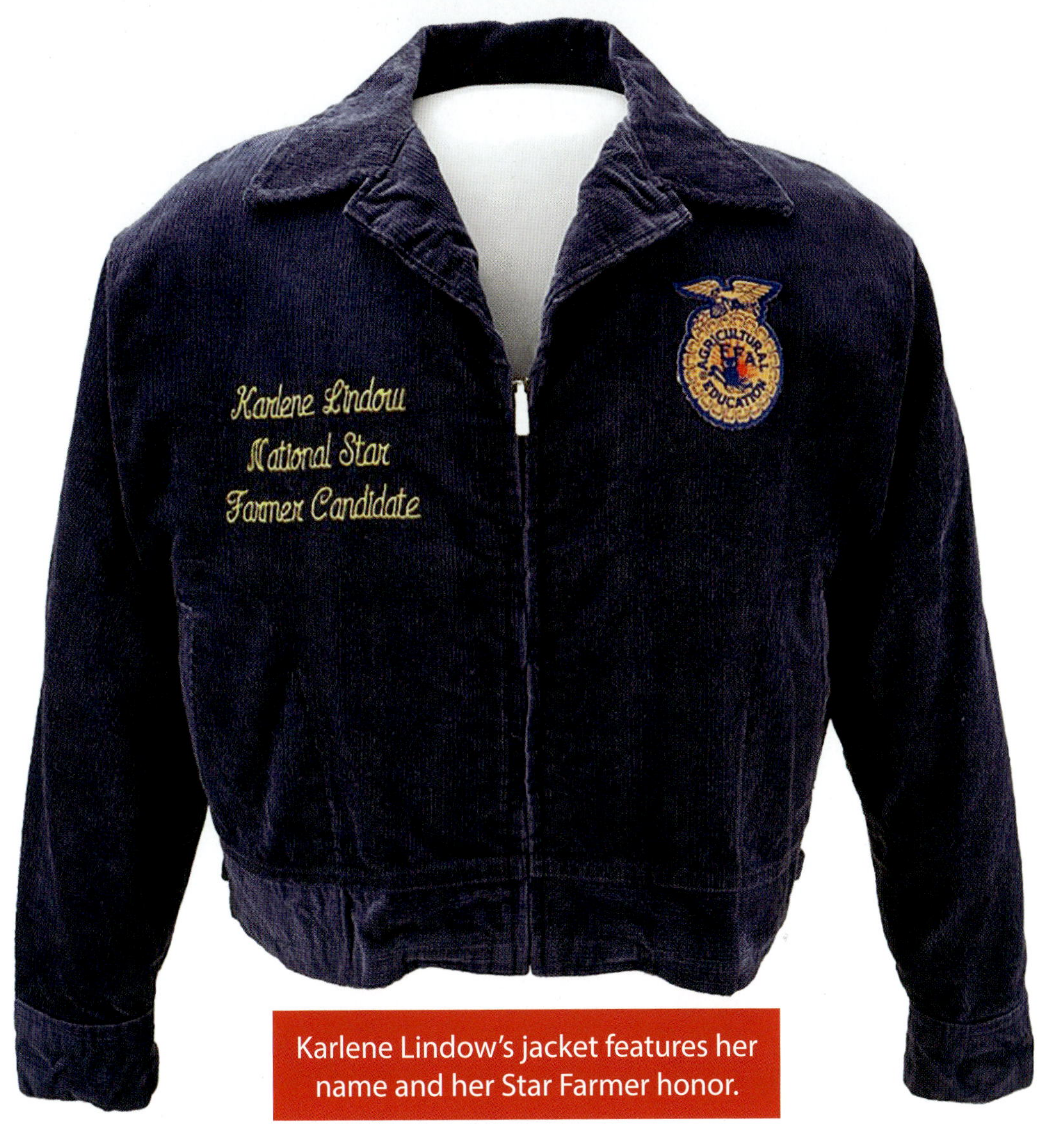

Karlene Lindow's jacket features her name and her Star Farmer honor.

Lindow's jacket is on display at the National Museum of American History in Washington, DC.

In 2003, Javier Moreno of Puerto Rico became the first national FFA president elected whose first language was not English. The year 2006 saw the National FFA Convention move to Indianapolis, Indiana. There were 54,489 attendees. By 2007, FFA had more than 500,000 members.

The 2014 Nebraska state convention brought thousands of FFA members to the capital, Lincoln.

2010s

The year 2013 brought another first for FFA at the national professional level. Sherene Donaldson became the first female national FFA executive secretary. Her roles included working with state FFA associations, tracking membership, and monitoring how the organization was doing. She reported to the FFA board of directors.

During the 2010s, the National FFA Convention moved again. It was held in Kentucky from 2013 to 2015. Then it moved back to Indiana in 2016.

That same year, the official dress code was updated. Female members were no longer required to wear skirts. Male and female members could wear their choice of skirts or pants.

Members could also wear any religious attire along with their official dress.

FFA continues to change. But it remains dedicated to agricultural education. Its membership is still growing, influencing hundreds of thousands of students each year.

The modern FFA dress code offers more flexibility than in the past.

THE PEOPLE OF FFA

Agricultural students across the United States participate in FFA. In 2022, there were more than 850,000 members. Of those members, 43 percent are female, 50 percent are male, and 0.5 percent are nonbinary. A further 5.9 percent did not disclose or report gender. The figures do not add up to exactly 100 percent due to rounding. White students make up 62 percent of membership, while 16 percent are Hispanic or Latino. Six percent of members are Black, 1 percent are American Indian or Alaska Native, and 1 percent are Asian, Hawaiian, or Pacific Islander. About 3 percent reported two or more races, and another 11 percent did not disclose race.

There are FFA chapters in all states. There are also chapters in Puerto Rico and in the US Virgin Islands, which are both territories of the United States. The states with the most members are Texas, California, Georgia, North Carolina, and Tennessee. Rural members make up 60 percent of membership. About 20 percent of members are in towns, 12 percent are in suburbs, and 7 percent are in cities. About 1 percent of members did not report a location.

Major FFA events draw thousands of members from across the United States.

A display at the Iowa State Fair showcased FFA jackets from each of the state's counties.

FFA is largely for high schoolers, while 4-H has more focus on activities for elementary-school kids.

Many FFA members started in 4-H, which is available to students younger than FFA allows. They later transitioned to FFA. Students in grades 5 through 12 who are enrolled in a school agricultural program can become FFA members. Before 2023, FFA membership started at grade 7. But it added grades 5 and 6 ahead of the 2023–2024 school year. Some states, such as Wisconsin and New Jersey, offered agricultural courses for these grades. However, many schools across the nation limited agricultural courses to grades 7 and up, in part because of a shortage of agricultural educators. This means that most FFA members are in grades 7 and up. After graduating from high school, students in college can join a collegiate FFA chapter.

Students join FFA to learn about agricultural career options, prepare for college, and study technology. Through FFA, they receive agricultural education. This prepares them for careers in not only agriculture but also science, education, horticulture, forestry, and many other fields.

As the organization's name suggests, FFA is geared toward training the next generation of the nation's farmers.

THE STRUCTURE OF FFA

There are three basic levels of FFA. The local level is the individual chapters, which are based out of schools. The chapters can exist in any school that includes agricultural education. Programs at local chapters teach students about raising livestock and growing crops. They also cover environmental and natural resources.

Chapter members elect student officers to lead them. Officer positions include president, vice president, secretary, and treasurer. The president's roles include coordinating activities for the chapter and representing

FFA members in North Dakota show off the plants they grew at their vocational school.

Wesley Dunham, vice president of his FFA chapter in Illinois, demonstrates a tool for draining water from a local recreational trail.

the chapter at events. The vice president stands in for the president if needed and makes a program of activities for the chapter. The secretary prepares materials for meetings, tracks member attendance, and handles communication within the chapter. The treasurer manages the chapter's funds and collects dues. An agricultural teacher from the school serves as the FFA adviser for the chapter. This adviser oversees the instruction of the chapter, provides training for student leaders, and coaches students who are entering competitions.

STATE LEVEL

A state FFA association oversees the local chapters within its state. These associations are usually part of a state's department of education. They offer programs to give members practice with public speaking, managing finances, solving problems, and more. State associations also hold yearly conventions for the members in their state. These conventions attract thousands of members and guests. The event can include

Indiana FFA vice president Julia Hamblen spoke at the inauguration ceremony for her state's governor in 2021.

FFA members may participate in state-level events, such as opening a state fair.

competitions, leadership workshops, and opportunities to meet college and business representatives.

State associations can also offer awards that are unique to their state. For example, Texas offers the John Justin Standard of the West Award. This is given to a student in each of the Texas regions who demonstrates a good work ethic, honesty, family values, helpfulness, and other traits. The winners receive a plaque and $500. A state winner is selected from those finalists, and that person receives a plaque and $2,500.

NATIONAL LEVEL

The National FFA Organization is a nonprofit organization. It oversees the state associations. It provides materials for various programs. The national organization also runs the National FFA Convention.

A board of directors and National FFA Officers work together to govern the organization. The board of directors

National FFA Officers and candidates may get the opportunity to meet the president of the United States. A group of them visited George W. Bush at the White House in 2008.

consists of adults, including representatives from the US Department of Education, officials from the National Council for Agricultural Education, and agricultural education teachers. National FFA Officers are student leaders. Each state can put forward no more than one candidate for the national FFA office every year. Delegates elect six national officers at the convention. The officers serve one-year terms.

In 2022, the Kansas FFA accepted a donation from Farmland, a company that sells pork products.

NATIONAL FOUNDATION

The National FFA Foundation raises funding for FFA. Most of its donations come from corporations. Some of the biggest donors are farming companies such as John Deere and Tractor Supply Company, which have donated more than $1 million. Individuals also contribute. The money is used to fund the National FFA Organization, give scholarships to students, and provide funding to chapters and state associations.

FFA PROGRAMS

There is a wide range of programs available through FFA. They can vary by state and by what is available locally. Regardless of location, participation in FFA fulfills three important parts of agricultural education. First, it involves classroom and laboratory instruction through schools. Second, it emphasizes the development of leadership skills and career preparation. And third, it incorporates hands-on work related to agriculture through a supervised agricultural experience (SAE).

FFA's many programs and activities offer fun, education, and useful training.

Every FFA member must have an SAE. The SAE helps students apply what they have learned in classroom lessons. SAEs are tailored to each student and are related to the field a student is most interested in. FFA and the National Council for Agricultural Education partnered to create the SAE for All program. This connection makes SAEs accessible to all students, including those who do not have access to active agricultural businesses. In this program, there are two broad categories of SAE: the foundational SAE and the immersion SAE.

Beekeeping is one way that FFA members can get hands-on experience with agriculture.

The financial aspects of farming are often just as important as what happens in the fields, so budgeting and saving are key skills for FFA members to learn.

FOUNDATIONAL SAE

All agricultural students complete a foundational SAE. This type of SAE helps students determine which agricultural careers best suit their skills and interests. The experience involves researching careers to identify what interests the student. Then the student works to develop skills, such as critical thinking and communication, needed for success in college and the workforce.

Then students learn how to manage their finances by practicing budgeting and saving. They learn about workplace safety and environmental management. They also gain an understanding of the agricultural industry as a whole, including how certain issues and trends affect different parts of the industry. Many of the activities for this kind of SAE happen outside of the classroom.

Helping out on a farm can give teens a better appreciation for the business of agriculture.

IMMERSION SAE

The foundational SAE continues throughout a student's time in an agricultural program. However, the initial work done for the foundational SAE prepares students for an immersion SAE. This SAE provides hands-on experience in the career the student wants to pursue. Students may do more than one immersion SAE throughout their years in an agricultural program. They can choose from at least one of five types of immersion SAEs. The first is a placement or internship. The second involves ownership or entrepreneurship. The third is about research. The fourth is a school-based enterprise. And the fifth immersion SAE is related to service learning.

PLACEMENT OR INTERNSHIP

In a placement or internship SAE, students gain experience in a career field by working as an employee or volunteering in the workplace. For example, students may work on a farm or in a food testing laboratory. They may also work for a nonprofit that is related to agriculture.

Some students may choose to do internships at locations such as feedlots. They can gain experience in feeding the animals or bookkeeping. A feedlot is a place where livestock, such as cattle, are kept in relatively small areas for their size and fed mainly grains to fatten them up for market. Feedlots are controversial because cattle's natural diet is grass. When fed grains, cattle may develop stomach issues, including ulcers and liver abscesses.

Feedlots are also called animal feeding operations.

Large feedlots have become one of many controversial issues in modern farming.

Due to the crowded conditions of feedlots, livestock are especially at risk of disease. They are often given antibiotics as a preventative measure rather than only as a treatment for an existing illness. Medical experts have concerns that using antibiotics in this way can cause the development of antibiotic-resistant bacteria, which are bacteria that no longer respond to antibiotics. This type of bacteria can be more deadly because it can't be treated.

At the same time, raising beef is an expensive process, and feedlots help farmers reduce costs. Grains digest more quickly than grass, and when this is combined with the cattle's low activity level, these animals reach slaughter weight much more quickly than pasture-fed cattle. Feedlot cattle are less likely to eat poisonous plants or fungi and to have nutritional deficiencies. Working in this kind of SAE gives students real-world experience that can help them shape their own views on farming practices.

Hands-on experience with cattle and other livestock can ensure FFA members are well-informed when it comes to the agriculture issues of the day.

OWNERSHIP AND ENTREPRENEURSHIP

Students who want to start their own business may choose the ownership and entrepreneurship SAE. The business must provide goods or services related to agriculture. There can be financial risk, as the student may invest money to produce a product that doesn't sell well enough to recover costs. However, this SAE also gives students business experience at every level, from developing products or services to managing funds and providing hands-on labor.

Auctioning meat they raised can provide FFA members with valuable business experience.

FFA member Kim Riley sold her prize-winning eggs at an event in West Virginia.

For example, some students choose to start an organic crop or meat business. Organic crops are crops that have been grown to meet many criteria. They must be grown in fields that do not use synthetic fertilizers or pesticides. They cannot be genetically modified, meaning they cannot have had their genes changed by means beyond natural reproduction. Organic meat comes from animals that have been fed organic foods entirely and have not received antibiotics or growth hormones.

In 2021, more than 8.6 million acres (3.5 million ha) of US farmland were dedicated to organic crops.

People choose organic foods over nonorganic ones for many reasons. Some reasons, such as the belief that organic foods are more nutritious, have little evidence to support them. Other reasons, such as organic foods being better for the environment, have more evidence. Because organic foods do not use pesticides that kill beneficial insects, they help maintain those insect populations. They also limit the consumer's exposure to pesticide residue and antibiotic-resistant bacteria. However, organic foods are often more expensive and spoil more quickly than nonorganic foods.

One organic SAE project could be growing organic crops in a window basket and selling them. Eventually, the student may raise enough money to be able to rent a field to grow more organic crops. In order to sell organic crops or meat, students must follow all the rules and regulations surrounding organic farming. Some states may offer grants to students who are conducting organic-farming SAEs. Students may use this money to rent or buy land. They may also use it to purchase equipment that will help them work more efficiently, such as irrigation systems, which help with watering.

RESEARCH

Some students select a research SAE. Students who choose this SAE conduct research that tries to answer a question or solve a problem related to agriculture. The research may support existing outcomes or provide new information. Students may uncover solutions and create new inventions.

There are three types of research SAEs. An experimental research SAE follows the scientific method. Students start with a hypothesis and then develop a research plan. They conduct research, collect data, come to a conclusion, and recommend further research. For example, students involved in this type of SAE may conduct a study on what type of feed works best for chickens.

Researching plant growth can help prepare FFA members for a scientific agricultural career.

Developing skills related to the scientific method can help students with problem solving in many industries beyond farming.

Surveying people about farming issues can help FFA members discover topics that might benefit from public education campaigns.

An analytical research SAE typically tries to answer a question of how or why something happens. The student collects data and studies it to arrive at an answer to the question. For example, a student might conduct a poll to see how the public views organic and nonorganic food. The results could help improve public education around food.

The invention research SAE involves developing a new product for the market. Students find a need, such as observing a gate that is difficult for one person to open and close. They might design and build a gate that is easier for one person to manage.

Research SAEs might deal with topics such as genetically modified organisms (GMOs). Some people are concerned that GMOs may be harmful when eaten. Most studies have suggested that GMOs do not have negative health consequences. FFA's position on GMOs is that these foods help a greater percentage of a crop survive to harvest. This is because GMOs have had genes modified that make them less desirable to pests or more resistant to herbicides used to kill weeds growing in the same field. For a research SAE involving GMOs, FFA students might conduct a survey with the general public to understand what the public knows about GMOs.

Organic food and GMOs are hot topics in agriculture, making them good subjects for FFA research projects.

SCHOOL-BASED ENTERPRISE

The school-based enterprise SAE involves working with other students, basing operations out of the school. The goal is to provide goods or services related to agriculture. Students might start a landscaping business. People could hire them to design landscaping for a yard or business, draw up

FFA members in Illinois gained hands-on experience with landscaping work in 2017.

Members of the FFA in Pennsylvania restored a John Deere tractor in 2007.

plans for the work, and select the types of plants to use. The students can then be hired to do the landscaping work.

Another option for students in this program could be a business repairing agricultural equipment. Some schools even have their own livestock farms. Local residents may purchase cattle, pigs, or other livestock and have students raise them to market weight.

SERVICE LEARNING

The fifth immersion SAE is the service-learning SAE. This type of SAE provides a service that benefits a group, organization, or individual. Students must raise funds if there will be expenses, organize the service, and carry it out. Students may work individually or in a group to complete this SAE.

Students participating in this type of SAE might volunteer to help plan and develop a city park. They might set up collection events for a local food bank. They could also grow food to donate to a charity organization.

Jamar Brown and other FFA members in South Carolina donated flowers to be planted at the state capitol.

FFA students in California helped a local nonprofit organization sort food donations.

Livestock competitions are a major part of FFA. These events give the public a chance to see the hard work of FFA members.

COMPETITIONS

FFA members might enter competitions as part of their SAEs or as additional activities. Starting at the local level, students can participate in career and leadership development events. These events give students a chance to apply classroom knowledge to real-world situations in a competitive environment. Some of these competitions are done individually, while others are done as teams. Students who do well at regional competitions can qualify for state-level competitions, which are often held at state fairs. State finalists have the opportunity to compete at the National FFA Convention.

One career development event is in agronomy. Teams of three or four members take exams where they identify seeds, insects, and crops. Tests may require team members to solve agricultural problems. Teams of three or four students can also compete by evaluating horse breeds such as Appaloosas, American Quarter Horses, or Morgans. The students rank the animals based on how closely they conform to breed standards. They can also judge horse performance events, such as western pleasure, English pleasure, or reining.

FFA members in California judged oranges at a citrus event in 2018.

Gabrielle Lemenager, an FFA member from Illinois, judges a hog competition.

When competing in livestock judging, teams of three or four evaluate beef cattle, sheep, goats, or swine for breeding or market. They judge weight, muscle thickness, and other traits that make the animals desirable for breeding or meat. Students can also compete in evaluating poultry and eggs.

In the tractor technician competition, teams examine parts of a tractor. They assess what servicing the parts need. Students may also repair malfunctions in tractors. They drive repaired tractors through a course, which they must complete within a time limit.

FFA members in Idaho drove their tractors to school in recognition of FFA Week in February 2014.

One leadership development event is the agricultural issues forum. Teams research all sides of an agricultural issue and present their findings and interpretations to judges. They must be able to answer questions the judges may have about the issue and their findings.

Another leadership development event is public speaking. Students give a six-to-eight-minute speech about agriculture. They are judged on how well they deliver the speech and answer judges' questions.

Whether FFA members are speaking to expert judges or elementary school classrooms, public speaking skills are valuable to develop.

NATIONAL FFA CONVENTION

The National FFA Convention is held annually in the fall. More than 69,000 people attended in 2022. Each state sends at least two student delegates, but the exact number varies based on the percentage of the national membership that state makes up. At the convention, delegates set membership dues. They elect the next National FFA Officers. They also make recommendations for changes to the organization.

State competition winners from career and leadership development events gather at the convention to

President Donald Trump was among the speakers at the 2018 National FFA Convention, which was held in Indianapolis, Indiana.

compete nationally. They might compete in public speaking events, presenting information about topics such as GMOs. Others compete in agronomy, horse evaluation, and various career development events. Winners in the national competitions receive cash prizes.

US Secretary of Agriculture Tom Vilsack, *left*, spoke with FFA members at the 2016 National FFA Convention.

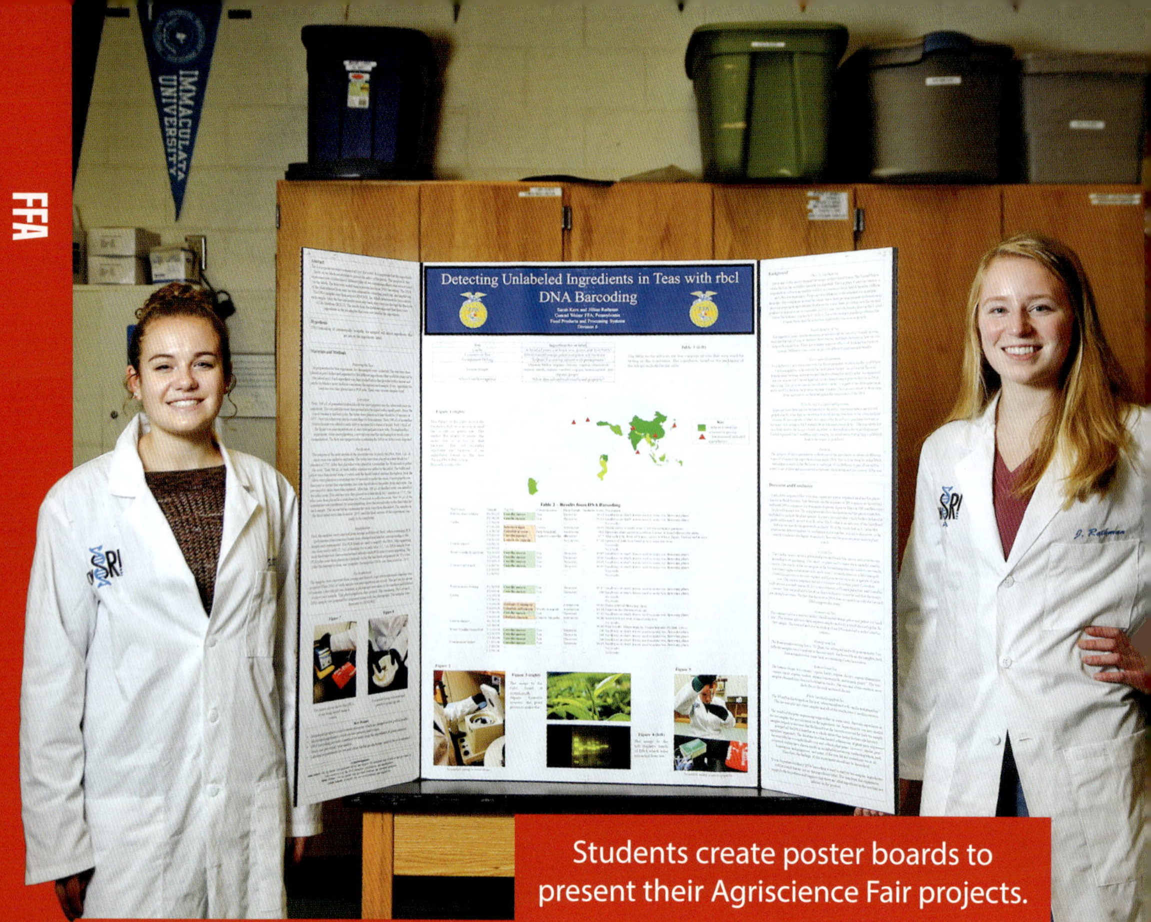

Students create poster boards to present their Agriscience Fair projects.

The National FFA Agriscience Fair also takes place at the convention. Students who won at state agriscience fairs can display their projects here. These students conduct scientific research and use technology to solve food, agriculture, and natural resource problems. They give a presentation on their findings to a panel of judges.

National awards are also given out at the convention. These include the American Star Farmer, American Star in Agribusiness, American Star in Agricultural Placement, and American Star in Agriscience awards. Only one student in the nation can receive each of these awards for the year.

Megan Campbell of Pennsylvania won a State Star in Agriscience award in 2013.

DEGREES

Besides awards, FFA students can work toward earning degrees. Students can apply for these when they have fulfilled the requirements. The Discovery Degree is for students in seventh and eighth grade. The requirements include becoming an FFA member, participating in at least one chapter activity that isn't during regular class time, and understanding agricultural careers and opportunities for starting businesses.

Starting with the Greenhand Degree, the remaining degrees build off each other. To apply for the Greenhand Degree, students must know and be able to explain many aspects of the FFA organization, such as the creed, mission, and motto.

For an activity outside of regular class time, FFA members might visit an elementary school to teach the students about animals.

FFA members must learn the rules associated with the FFA jacket, such as displaying the FFA emblem and always fastening the zipper to the top.

They must also understand the correct use of the FFA jacket, the organization's history, and the chapter constitution and bylaws.

Requirements for receiving the Chapter Degree include having received the Greenhand Degree and having had 180 hours of classroom instruction on agriculture at the ninth-grade level or higher. Students must have an active SAE. They must have either earned and invested $150 or worked for 45 hours outside the classroom.

FFA members in California serve their community by fixing a greenhouse at their high school.

After earning the Chapter Degree, students can work toward the State Degree. This degree's requirements include being an active FFA member for the past 24 months and having had 360 hours of classroom agricultural instruction. The required amount earned and invested and the number of hours worked can vary by state. Some states, such as Minnesota and Kansas, require at least $2,000 and 600 hours. Other states, such as Oregon, require at least $1,500 and 500 hours. Students must have completed 25 hours of community service, and they must have participated in a certain number of activities above the chapter level. The exact number varies by state.

To be eligible for the top degree, the American Degree, students must have received the State Degree. They must have graduated high school at least 12 months before the National FFA Convention, which is when the award is presented. The student must have earned at least $10,000 and invested $7,500, or earned and invested $2,000 and worked 2,250 hours. The person must have good grades and have completed at least 50 hours of community service.

Earning good grades is an important part of achievement within FFA.

FFA INFLUENCE

FFA has influenced individuals, communities, and the agricultural industry. It prepares youth for careers that will help the nation. It does this by developing students' leadership skills. Students can attend conferences that teach them about leadership, and they can hold offices in the organization that allow them to practice these skills.

Participation in FFA can instill a good work ethic. Students work hard to achieve various goals, such as earning degrees

National FFA vice president Abrah Meyer is among the many FFA members who have gained valuable leadership experience within the organization.

FFA members develop friendships while learning together and working toward common goals.

or winning competitions. And by doing foundational SAEs, students learn about various agricultural jobs. They can decide on a career path and begin preparing for it while they are still in high school. That preparation includes gaining hands-on experience. Students learn how to handle animals. They learn how to repair and operate tractors. These skills can help them in agricultural jobs.

The National FFA Convention, along with state and local events, gives students opportunities to network with businesses. They learn about what businesses are looking for in employees and discover companies they might enjoy working for or with. Businesses have noted that FFA programs help students develop communication and leadership skills, which allow them to thrive in an employment setting.

FFA also helps students develop as individuals, allowing them to offer fresh ideas that can help a company grow

Members of FFA may have the chance to meet with government leaders, such as Supreme Court justice Brett Kavanaugh, *center*.

FFA provides valuable education about agriculture to the general public, including information about water usage on farms.

in a way it could not otherwise. Through scholarships, FFA enables more students to receive quality education. And through grants, it helps students start up their SAEs, which can become businesses.

EDUCATION

FFA helps teach student members about agriculture. But it also provides many educational resources for the public. FFA's website includes educational videos that anyone can access for free. For example, the #SpeakAg Dialogues videos include panel discussions about issues in agriculture today, such as sustainable food production, whether current herbicides will remain effective at controlling weeds in the future, water shortages, and struggles for beginning farmers.

Project Carbonview helps producers of ethanol, a fuel made from corn, track carbon emissions across the entire process, from planting to producing fuel.

The FFA Blue 365 videos showcase industry and agricultural technology leaders, highlighting cutting-edge developments in agriculture. Topics include new processes in regenerative agriculture, which is the practice of rotating between multiple types of crops in order to help prevent pest infestations and avoid draining the soil of nutrients. It also covers ways that researchers are reducing carbon emissions in farming. For example, the companies Bayer, Bushel, and Amazon started Project Carbonview, in which researchers partner with farmers to analyze and lower carbon emissions. This enables farmers to take advantage of financial incentives for having low emissions.

Sometimes chapters also help with community education and preserve local history. In 2021, members of Tennessee's Scotts Hill FFA Chapter were learning about FFA's history. They began to question why so little was known about the NFA. Their adviser encouraged them to investigate and see what they could learn. As a result, they were able to uncover information about their local NFA chapter and found an NFA jacket, which they framed and hung alongside their collection of FFA jackets. They also planned to interview former members of the local NFA chapter to expand the official historical record for their community.

Some FFA members have studied and recorded important parts of NFA history.

SERVING THE COMMUNITY

Through degrees and chapter activities, students are encouraged to serve their communities. They see the beneficial impact they can have on the world. The last three words of the FFA motto are "living to serve," and FFA members put this into practice in many ways. Chapters can organize their own service projects at any time.

In addition, clubs might participate in the two National Days of Service, once in February and once in October. This work might be as simple as boosting community morale. In February 2023, the Morgan FFA chapter in Ohio visited 50 farmers, gave them doughnuts, and

Shelbie Huth cuts a piece of wood for a construction project that she and fellow Texas FFA members are completing at their high school.

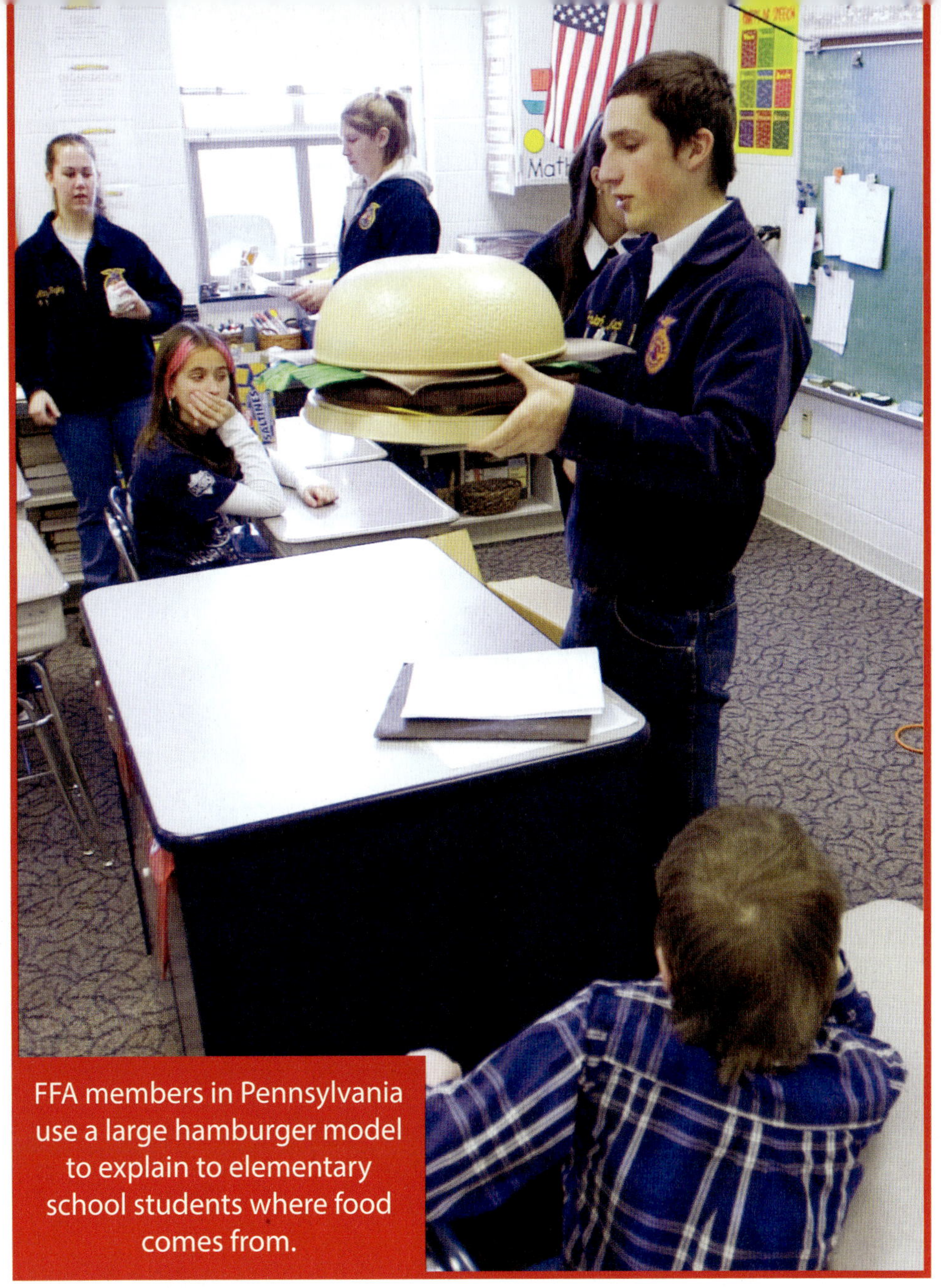

FFA members in Pennsylvania use a large hamburger model to explain to elementary school students where food comes from.

told them how much they appreciated the farmers' hard work. Some students take service even further through a service-based SAE. FFA offers grants to students who need funding for such SAEs.

Helping out with farm chores can be a way for FFA members to raise funds.

Some chapters, such as the Delphi FFA chapter in Indiana, fundraise by hiring out members for eight-hour workdays. Along with helping the chapter receive funding, this also helps people in the community. Residents can hire students to bale hay, help with livestock, or do other jobs that people might not be able to do on their own. The community members then donate money to the chapter.

Chapters may look for creative ways to interest others in agriculture. During the COVID-19 pandemic, many children had to stay home. Many of their usual activities had been canceled. Iowa's Belmond-Klemme FFA chapter partnered with Trees Forever, an environmental group, to make and distribute garden starter kits to help youth pass their time at home. The kits contained soil, seeds, and instructions for how to grow the crops.

Encouraging younger kids to garden helps FFA members promote an interest in agriculture for younger generations.

SAVING ANIMALS

An FFA student's SAE can help the community. For example, several chapters have made disaster plans for the animals in their communities. The Gridley FFA chapter in California created a disaster plan for livestock in 2017. Members were able to put this plan into use the very next year when the Camp Fire started in the state. As towns nearby were evacuated due to the deadly wildfire, the chapter members worked quickly to set up panels and pens at their local fairgrounds. Some chapter members drove trailers to properties near the fire to load up horses, sheep, pigs, and other animals and haul them to safety at the fairgrounds. Others fed and watered the animals when they reached safety. Some students also helped treat injured animals.

With devastating wildfires becoming more common, FFA members can play a role in protecting livestock during these disasters.

Rising waters from Hurricane Florence in 2018 flooded a North Carolina hog farm. Members of FFA are getting involved in finding solutions for keeping livestock safe.

Other chapters have used their schools as evacuation centers for pets during natural disasters, such as hurricanes. The Sarasota Vo-Ag FFA chapter cared for animals during Hurricane Irma in 2017. Members followed their disaster plan, setting up kennels, feeding and watering the animals, and practicing disinfection protocols. They also received training from the American Red Cross and the Florida State Animal Response Coalition so they could keep the animals safe and healthy. Not only did this help residents who could not bring their pets with them while they temporarily evacuated, but it also helped prepare FFA students who had an interest in veterinary careers.

An FFA group in Michigan organized a day of service to help clean up their high school's landscaping.

SERVING AT CONVENTIONS

State and national conventions are another time when FFA members help communities. In 2018, 800 students at Georgia's state convention participated in service projects. They helped out at 12 different sites. One site was the Rescue Mission of Middle Georgia. This organization helps people who are experiencing homelessness, domestic violence, addiction, and other situations to recover and get the resources they need. FFA volunteers spent the day planting gardens and weeding raised garden beds. The organization uses the gardens to help feed people in their programs.

Students also get the chance to serve the community at the National FFA Convention. There were nearly 20 volunteer opportunities at the 2023 event. At several parks, students worked to remove invasive species, develop landscaping, plant bulbs, collect and plant native seeds, and plant trees. Other students volunteered at food banks or food pantries, organizing and stocking shelves, repackaging bulk products, and cleaning. Some students got to work on repairs for a historical farmstead based on those from the 1930s. The volunteers restored farm tools, prepared the garden for winter, and readied the historical farmhouse for winter events.

FFA members volunteer to educate young students about the basics of agriculture.

JOINING FFA

Students who want to join FFA must be enrolled in an agricultural education program at school. Not all schools have these programs. If students are in such a program, they can check with the school to see if it has an FFA chapter. If the school has an agricultural education program but does not have a chapter, students might be allowed to join a different school's chapter. People can use the Chapter Locator feature on the FFA website to find a nearby chapter. They may also need to contact the state's FFA agency to check the rules for joining a chapter that is in a different school. The chapter adviser can help with the membership application.

In 2010, FFA members marched with an elaborate float to promote the organization at the Tournament of Roses parade in Los Angeles.

Membership in FFA has been a fun and rewarding experience for millions of youth.

Students in a school with an agricultural program may also ask the school to help start an FFA chapter. This process includes selecting FFA officers and drafting a chapter constitution. The school must then submit an application to the state agency.

Individual students joining a chapter must pay the membership dues to the National FFA Organization. In 2023, the dues were $7 per member. In addition, state agencies and local chapters may each have their own dues. There are additional costs for activities, conventions, and SAEs, but scholarships are sometimes available.

GLOSSARY

advocate
To support or argue for a cause.

alumni
People who have graduated from a program or school.

auction
The sale of property to the highest bidder.

bale
To gather and tie up hay.

bookkeeping
Recording the money and transactions of a business.

compensate
To provide a comparable amount, or to balance.

delegate
A person representing a group, such as at a convention.

economy
The money, goods, and services of an area.

emission
A substance, such as a gas, that has been released into the air.

foundation
An organization that offers grants to organizations or individuals.

grant
Money given for a specific purpose.

invasive species
A species that has been introduced to an area where it is not native and has caused native species to decline.

lease
To rent something.

organism
A living thing, such as a plant or an animal.

pandemic
A disease that affects a large percentage of a population across a wide geographic area.

protocol
A set of rules of behavior for a situation.

segregate
To separate groups based on traits, such as race.

slaughter
To kill livestock in order to harvest the meat.

sustainability
The state of a resource being renewable and not likely to be used up.

TO LEARN MORE

FURTHER READINGS

Castaldo, Nancy. *Ultimate Food Atlas*. National Geographic Kids, 2020.

Henzel, Cynthia Kennedy. *Jobs in Agriculture*. Abdo, 2024.

Lim, Angela. *The Crop Encyclopedia*. Abdo, 2025.

ONLINE RESOURCES

To learn more about 4-H and FFA, please visit **abdobooklinks.com** or scan this QR code. These links are routinely monitored and updated to provide the most current information available.

INDEX

PHOTO CREDITS

Cover Photos: Smith Collection/Gado/Archive Photos/Getty Images, front (4-H pin); Jeffrey Greenberg/Universal Images Group/Getty Images, front (boy with chicken); Chip Somodevilla/Getty Images News/Getty Images, front (Iowa fair ribbon); Lauren A. Little/MediaNews Group/Reading Eagle/Getty Images, front (girl with cows); Harold Hoch/MediaNews Group/Reading Eagle/Getty Images, front (FFA patch); Prairie View A&M University/Historically Black Colleges and Universities/Getty Images, front (4-H girls); Shutterstock Images, front (Minnesota fair ribbon, vegetables, rope), back (4-H sign, stamp)

Interior Photos: Smith Collection/Gado/Archive Photos/Getty Images, 1 (left); Shutterstock Images, 1 (right), 5, 30, 36–37, 39, 52, 52–53, 54–55, 55, 58, 60–61, 67, 85, 87, 88, 94–95, 95, 131, 142, 144, 148–149, 152, 153, 175, 176 180; Mert Alper Dervis/Anadolu/Getty Images, 2–3; J. R. Hamlin/Archive Photos/Getty Images, 6; Keystone-France/Gamma-Keystone/Getty Images, 7; Iowa Digital Library, 8; Lewis W. Hine/Buyenlarge/Archive Photos/Getty Images, 9; Library of Congress, 10–11, 110; Maginel Wright Barney/National War Garden Commission/Library of Congress, 11; Underwood Archives/Archive Photos/Getty Images, 12–13; Corbis Historical/Getty Images, 14; Bettmann/Getty Images, 15, 16, 22–23; Jerry Cooke/The Chronicle Collection/Getty Images, 17; Prairie View A&M University/Historically Black Colleges and Universities/Getty Images, 18, 19, 20–21, 22, 24, 25; John Prieto/Denver Post/Getty Images, 26; Greg White/Fairfax Media Archives/Getty Images, 27; Jerry Holt/Star Tribune/Getty Images, 28; Jonathan Deal/News Courier/AP Images, 29; John Patriquin/Portland Press Herald/Getty Images, 31; Bruce Bisping/Star Tribune/Getty Images, 32–33, 62; Brandy Taylor/iStockphoto, 33, 42; Katherine Frey/The Washington Post/Getty Images, 34; Ben Hasty/MediaNews Group/Reading Eagle/Getty Images, 35, 90, 154–155, 162–163, 168, 179; Michael Dames/National 4-H Council/Getty Images Entertainment/Getty Images, 37; Renee Jones Schneider/Star Tribune/Getty Images, 38; Steve Jennings/WireImage/Getty Images, 40; Christin Lola/iStockphoto, 41; Alan Murray/Herald Journal/AP Images, 42–43; Amy Toensing/Getty Images News/Getty Images, 44; Kathryn Scott Osler/Denver Post/Getty Images, 45; Tim Leedy/MediaNews Group/Reading Eagle/Getty Images, 46, 60, 84; Lewis Geyer/Digital First Media/Boulder Daily Camera/MediaNews Group/Getty Images, 47; Lea Suzuki/San Francisco Chronicle/Hearst Newspapers/Getty Images, 48; Natalia Fedosova/Shutterstock Images, 49; Vespasian/Alamy, 50; Derek Davis/Portland Press Herald/Getty Images, 51; J. J. Gouin/Shutterstock Images, 56; Steve Karnowski/AP Images, 57; Jeoffrey Guillemard/Bloomberg/Getty Images, 59; Jeff Greenberg/Universal Images Group/Getty Images, 63; Hum Images/Alamy, 64; Gregory Rec/Portland Press Herald/Getty Images, 65; University of Arkansas Division of Agriculture, 66, 68–69; Susan L. Angstadt/MediaNews Group/Reading Eagle/Getty Images, 70, 74; Kelly Schnoor/The Norfolk Daily News/AP Images, 71; Lauren A. Little/MediaNews Group/Reading Eagle/Getty Images, 72; Jeffrey Greenberg/Universal Images Group/Getty Images, 73, 187; Mike McCleary/Bismarck Tribune/AP Images, 74–75; iStockphoto, 76–77, 145, 150; Steve Russell/Toronto Star/Getty Images, 77; Dmytro Flisak/Shutterstock Images, 78; Fertnig/E+/Getty Images, 79; Zoran Zeremski/Shutterstock Images, 80; Jasmine Sahin/Shutterstock Images, 81; Nicholas J. Klein/Shutterstock Images, 82; Alex Edelman/AFP/Getty Images, 83; View Reiner Voë/picture-alliance/dpa/AP Images, 86; David Joles/Star Tribune/Getty Images, 89; Scott Olson/Getty Images News/Getty Images, 91; Brianna Soukup/Portland Press Herald/Getty Images, 92–93; Stuart Villanueva/Bryan College Station Eagle/AP Images, 96; Edwin Remsberg/VWPics/AP Images, 97; IUPUI University Library Special Collections and Archives, 98, 102–103, 105, 107, 108, 111, 114, 115, 117, 118–119, 120, 121, 122, 123, 176–177; IUPUI University Library, Ruth Lilly Special Collections and Archives, 99, 100, 104; Heritage Art/Heritage Images/Hulton Archive/Getty Images, 101; John Kelly/The Washington Post/Getty Images, 106; Universal History Archive/Universal Images Group/Getty Images, 109; Everett Collection/Shutterstock Images, 112; National Archives, 113; Los Angeles Examiner/USC Libraries/Corbis Historical/Getty Images, 116; Beth A. Keiser/AP Images, 124; Karlene Krueger/National Museum of American History, 125; Eric Gregory/Lincoln Journal Star/AP Images, 126; Rob Schultz/Wisconsin State Journal/AP Images, 127; Nicholas Kamm/AFP/Getty Images, 128, 164; Chip Somodevilla/Getty Images News/Getty Images, 129; Barrett Stinson/The Grand Island Independent/AP Images, 130; Cleo Cantlon/Minot Daily News/AP Images, 132; Jim Bowling/Herald & Review/AP Images, 132–133; Darron Cummings/AP Images, 134; Chris O'Meara/AP Images, 134–135; Aude Guerrucci/Getty Images News/Getty Images, 136–137; Travis Heying/Farmland/AP Images, 138; Harold Hoch/MediaNews Group/Reading Eagle/Getty Images, 139; Natalie Kolb/MediaNews Group/Reading Eagle/Getty Images, 140, 166; Nicky Lloyd/iStockphoto, 141; Paula Scavarelli/Shutterstock Images, 142–143; Jeff Gentner/AP Images, 146, 147; Jaclyn Vernace/Shutterstock Images, 150–151; Samantha McDaniel-Ogletree/Jacksonville Journal Courier/AP Images, 154; Mary Ann Chastain/AP Images, 156; Elias Funez/The Union/AP Images, 156–157; Andy Carpenean/Laramie Boomerang/AP Images, 158; Chieko Hara/The Porterville Recorder/AP Images, 159; Craig F. Walker/Denver Post/Getty Images, 160; Ashley Smith/Times-News/AP Images, 161; Kris Vance/USDA, 165; Jeremy Drey/MediaNews Group/Reading Eagle/Getty Images, 167; Ken Ruinard/Anderson Independent-Mail/AP Images, 169; Stephen Osman/Los Angeles Times/Getty Images, 170; Daniel Hoz/Shutterstock Images, 171; Mike Lawrence/The Gleaner/AP Images, 172; Allen J. Schaben/Los Angeles Times/Getty Images, 173; Tom Williams/CQ Roll Call/AP Images, 174; Emree Weaver/The Victoria Advocate/AP Images, 178; Juliya Shangarey/Shutterstock Images, 180–181; Tom Reichner/Shutterstock Images, 182; Alex Wroblewski/Bloomberg/Getty Images, 183; Ken Stevens/The Muskegon Chronicle/AP Images, 184; Gary Emord-Netzley/The Messenger-Inquirer/AP Images, 185; Marie Appert/iStockphoto, 186

ABDOBOOKS.COM
Published by Abdo Reference, a division of ABDO, PO Box 398166, Minneapolis, Minnesota 55439.

Printed in China.
052024
092024

Editor: Arnold Ringstad
Series Designer: Colleen McLaren
Production Designers: Karli Kruse, Laura Kuchar

LIBRARY OF CONGRESS CONTROL NUMBER: 2023949526

PUBLISHER'S CATALOGING-IN-PUBLICATION DATA
Names: Dinmont, Kerry, author.
Title: The 4-H and FFA encyclopedia / by Kerry Dinmont
Description: Minneapolis, Minnesota: Abdo Reference, 2025 | Series: Farming encyclopedias | Includes online resources and index.
Identifiers: ISBN 9781098294335 (lib. bdg.) | ISBN 9798384913603 (ebook)
Subjects: LCSH: 4-H clubs--Juvenile literature. | Future Farmers of America--Juvenile literature. | Young farmers' clubs--Juvenile literature. | Agriculture--Juvenile literature. | Farming--Juvenile literature. | Encyclopedias and dictionaries--Juvenile literature.
Classification: DDC 630.62--dc23